# We Made Plans

## Author La Onque Chavette

# We Made Plans

ISBN: 978-1-7341337-0-7

Published by Ellis Industries

## Contents

# We Made Plans

# La Onque Chavette

## PROLOGUE

**R**ACQUEL AMANI WILSON HAD THE BEST FRIENDS ever! They often made plans to do various things together from the time they were very little, in elementary school, through adulthood. Kelly, Brandon, Candice, Mo, and Sydney were Racquel's besties. That's an excessive number of best friends to have, but Racquel met each of her friends at different stages in her life and, like a hoarder, she refused to discard any of her friendships. She always chose to believe they would be friends FOREVER.

Racquel and Brandon Lamar Freeman attended Benjamin Franklin Elementary School in Jamisville, Delaware and had been friends practically since kindergarten. They saw each other at their very best and worst moments. It was Racquel who remembered, and never let Brandon forget, the time he ate white chalk pretending it was the candy cigarettes they sold at the corner stores back in the day. She remembered him holding the chalk the same way his dad held his cigarettes, and then taking bites of the chalk while some classmates said, "Ewww Brandon" and others giggled at his silliness. Racquel didn't know and didn't want to know how chalk tasted but Brandon ate two pieces of chalk so they must have tasted pretty good.

Not too long after eating the chalk, Brandon felt his mouth water and a lump in his throat. He had a distressed look on his face as he turned the color of a sienna crayon. His eyes bulged a little.

6

## La Onque Chavette

He covered his mouth and tried to swallow hard a few times. Then it happened. He violently vomited the chalk, despite trying his best to hold it in. He was missing his two front teeth and the vomit easily poured out of his mouth, puddled in his hand and spilled over to the floor in a loud, disgusting splat that echoed through the classroom.

The residue left a white foam around his mouth, resembling a rabid animal. Their teacher, Ms. Dalakian, almost fainted when she laid eyes on him. She screamed, "Oh my God! Brandon what did you eat?" Then she violently patted him on the back as if he were choking on something. Racquel laughed so hard that she got in trouble for not having "compassion" for a fellow classmate who was sick. Ms. Dalakian wrote a note to Racquel's parents about her behavior and lack of sympathy for her classmate and sent it home. It was the first of several notes various teachers would send home over the years.

Racquel just thought it served Brandon right for trying to be funny by eating chalk. "Who eats chalk?", Racquel thought to herself. Even at a young age Racquel knew better but Brandon would prove to make poor decisions, and make them often.

Brandon was hilarious to be around, sweet, eventually had a great smile when his adult teeth grew in, and overall, a good person. He just made extremely questionable choices. Ultimately, Racquel thought he did it more for laughs than anything else. Brandon could always count on her to laugh so hard at some of the ridiculous things he did that they both got into trouble for it. Their teachers would often say, "Racquel, since you think it's so funny, you can go to the office with him!" For which her laughter stopped and the begging for mercy began. Sometimes Racquel wouldn't be involved at all, but still managed to get into trouble. It was a classic case of guilt by association. Racquel really didn't mind because Brandon made the school days easier to get through. If they had the same teachers from year to year, they were happy.

Racquel was also the only real friend to Brandon when his Dad moved out and left the family. It was truly a traumatic time for him in the fourth grade. Brandon thought everything was his fault because he was always getting into so much trouble. It took a while for Brandon to accept that his Dad's leaving was not his fault and when he realized it, he went hard on acting up in class. The Principal threatened to separate Racquel and Brandon, by putting him in a separate classroom for disruptive behaviors, but he managed to get it together.

Brandon needed a good friend during those turbulent times and Racquel turned out to be the friend he depended on. He would often go to her house for dinner and just sit and talk with her family. Racquel's Dad didn't mind because he knew Brandon needed a trustworthy, male figure he could relate to. Brandon became a part of the family over the years; an extension of Racquel's family. He even took day trips with them every summer.

## CHAPTER ONE

**R**ACQUEL AND BRANDON MET KELLY H. (don't ask her about her middle name) Cook in about sixth grade. Kelly was more reserved than Brandon. She brought the balance Racquel needed instead of dealing with Brandon's daily shenanigans. Kelly was smart, quiet, and a devout Christian. She was raised in a two-parent household and was the oldest child of four siblings. Her parents seemed to have a lot of money because she had a room with her very own attached bathroom, called a princess suite. She didn't have to share the 3rd bathroom in the house with her other siblings, which was a good thing because they were all boys. They had 3.5 baths in the one house so that welcomed guests could simply use the half bath on the first floor and not venture up to the bedrooms and bathrooms on the second floor. Kelly's friends, however, were not allowed to use the half bathroom. They had to go home and use their own bathroom. Her mom would ask, "Don't you live right around the corner?" When whomever replied, "yes", then she would say, "well go use your own bathroom baby, we gotta pay the water bill just like your people do!"

Kelly's parents had the coolest basement too. They had a theater room and another space with a pool table, air hockey and a video game. Their house was cool, but the Cooks were very particular about who could come in and out of the house. They said things like, "don't be inviting the devil into your home". At least, Kelly's mom was overheard saying that. Usually, family members and only a few select friends were allowed to visit and enjoy the fruits of their labor. Racquel and Brandon speculated as to what exactly their "labor" was. They thought that maybe Kelly's parents worked for the CIA and conducted undercover operations out of a secret room in the house.

After a couple of years, Racquel was eventually able to win them over. Her first visit to the inside of Kelly's house was when her parents hosted a small group of girls for the 8th grade dance and all the girls left from Kelly's house in a stretch Hummer limo. They were allowed to arrive a few hours early before they were scheduled to be at the dance. Kelly's parents served a light mixture of finger foods like ham and cheese roll ups, pepperoni pinwheels, pastry puffs, a veggie platter and a fruit tray along with chips, bottled water and other clear drinks. Racquel noticed that Kelly's mom always served light colored drinks and never the flavorful red, blue or purple drinks. Kelly said that her mom didn't want guests to spill any colored drinks on her light beige carpets. Racquel thought, "oh, that makes sense."

Kelly's mom was very particular about her house and keeping it orderly. She prided herself on a clean, fresh smelling home. Everyone had their tasks and chores that they were responsible for. There was no such thing as spring cleaning at her house. They cleaned daily, weekly and sometimes monthly, but not seasonally. At some point, Kelly's dad suggested, interviewed and hired a cleaning service but her Mom fired them after the first visit. She said the towels they used to clean with made her bathroom smell like a public toilet. The whole family had to go through and thoroughly clean up the very same day. That was the day Racquel learned, from Kelly's Dad, that even the best and most devout Christians sometimes fall short of the glory and curse a little bit, followed by repentance and prayer.

# La Onque Chavette

There was a friend of the families at the house for the 8th grade dance who was a makeup artist. She gave all the 8th grade girls a conservative, subtle makeover with tinted lip-gloss but no real lip color, a dab of blush on their cheeks, blended well and a hint of eyeshadow from a neutral, natural palette. Kelly couldn't wear real makeup until she was in high school so that meant no eyeliner for Kelly, not even on such an auspicious occasion. When they settled into the stretch Hummer limo, Racquel put her own eyeliner on and thought to herself, "well, they're not the boss of me."

We Made Plans

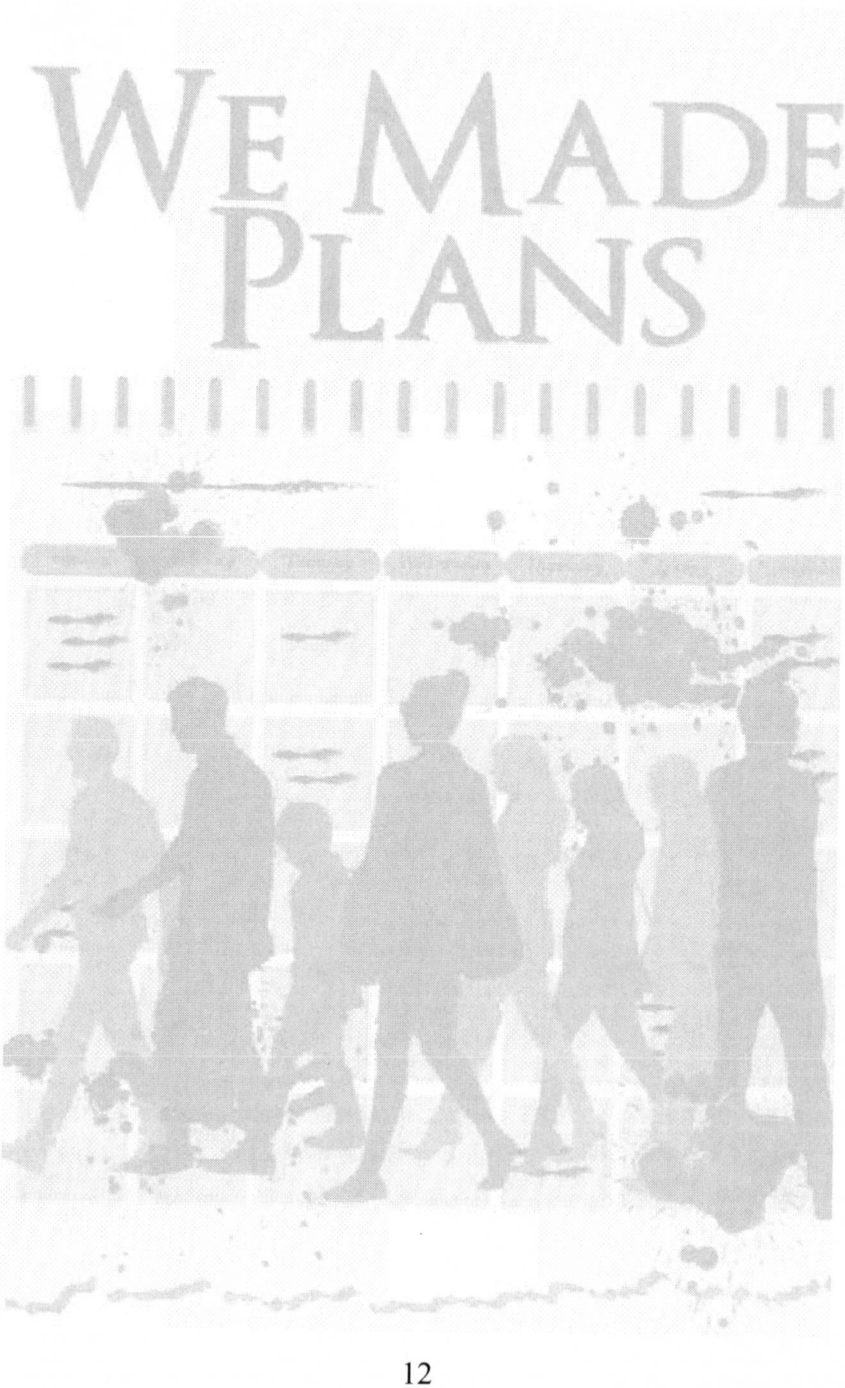

## CHAPTER TWO

**B**RANDON, KELLY AND RACQUEL entered high
school together.  They were all good friends and were
excited even though Brandon wasn't allowed in Kelly's
home.   Racquel thought there was a correlation between his
mischievous shenanigans and Kelly's parent's thoughts on devils in
the house.  Nonetheless, they were good friends, headed to high
school together unaware of what the next four years would hold, but
confident that their friendships were strong and that they would be
friends FOREVER!

Morton Thomas Goodwin, lovingly referred to as Mo, blasted
on the scene the second marking period of their Freshman year of
high school.  He was tall, brown skinned, and looked as if his
dreadlocks had been in for a year or so.  They had transitioned from
sticking straight up on his head to gently flopping down around his
slightly chiseled face.  He had light brown eyes but not quite hazel.
When the sunlight hit them, they sparkled like diamonds.  He was
an athlete, so he had a nice build which just got better over time.

Mo was the youngest of three siblings.  He was the baby of
the family and everyone could tell.  His mother adored him and
spoiled him rotten.  She would always ask him how he was doing by
saying, "how's Mommy's baby?"  She made sure he ate and never
let his stomach growl for more than two minutes.  If Mo said he was
hungry, she made something for him to eat.  If she couldn't make

him something to eat, then she gave him money or transferred money into his account so that he could eat right away. Sunday dinners at Mo's house were a big to-do because his Mom loved to cook. She made huge dinners to feed her family of five and whoever else stopped by on a Sunday afternoon. She took great pleasure in watching people enjoy her food and she thoroughly enjoyed the company.

Mo's Dad did a lot for him and defended everything he did at all costs. One-time Mo and a classmate were playing in class and knocked a computer over. Technically they bumped into it, the plug was snatched out of the wall and as it came crashing to the ground, Mo caught it with his hands, shin and foot. It did not touch the ground. It did not break, and it rebooted after being plugged back in.

The Vice Principal wanted to suspend Mo and the classmate, Tony, but Mo's Dad came to the school and shut it all down. He successfully argued the ridiculousness of taking a child away from precious classroom instruction for a one-day suspension for something so minor, that did not result in any damage or costs to the school, nor irreparable harm to anyone else. He even made the VP take the negative mark off Tony's record too since he was removing it from Mo's record. That was the fair thing to do. Mo's Dad was serious about treating others fairly and instilled that quality in all his children.

Mo and his brother and sister were well disciplined and rarely got into trouble. If by chance one got into trouble with Mo, it wasn't a bad thing because his Dad was no joke and spit fire when he spoke to people of authority. Not that he yelled, cursed, or fought anyone. He really didn't have to. He had a strong authoritative voice that made other people's children stop dead in their tracks if he yelled. He was also a book worm, impressively articulate and was law school bound for some time before he married and had kids.

Unlike Brandon, on the rare occasion Mo got into trouble, it was for things relevant to his athleticism, like running in the high school hallway because he was late for class and taking out a teacher, Mrs. Gibson, who walked right into his path. That was a mess! Mrs. Gibson was petite, and Mo knocked her about five to ten feet from where she was standing at impact. The kids, in the front of her class, yelled, "OOOOOOO" and called the front office because she was HURT. Mo was suspended for a day after that incident, with no protest from his Dad. Mo felt horrible. It didn't help that Mrs. Gibson was out sick for two days afterwards and came back to school with an exaggerated limp for about a week.

Mo grew into a big guy with a big heart, but you had to get past his look that grew slightly menacing by their senior year of high school. He was big and his dreadlocks were well past his shoulders and long enough to tie back with other dreadlocks. He didn't smile much but he laughed hard with his few chosen friends, which were some of his trusted teammates, Racquel, Brandon and Kelly. He would defend them as fiercely as his Dad defended him, no matter what. He had many of his Dad's characteristics and was a good guy.

Brandon, Kelly, Mo and Racquel made it through high school together the best of friends. There were some awkward first kisses, uncomfortable moments of "I like you but ...we're best buds. I don't want to mess up our friendship", to "what girl are you messing with now?", to "he is no good for you, he's a dog, don't mess with him". Everyone was concerned about the others' love life but never ventured into being the love of the others' lives. They just barked unsolicited instructions on who to avoid. They never gave a nod to anyone good. If there was silence on a person of interest, that meant they were probably ok…for now.

Kelly was accepted to an Ivy League college in New York just as her parents had instilled in her from her youth. She was the oldest and she had no other option but to set the bar for her brothers. She was a high achiever, not quite an over-achiever. Her parents had reasonable expectations for their first-born child, and she worked hard to make her parents proud and to please God. All her decisions revolved around this and she often preached to Racquel and especially to Brandon about choices and decisions. Kelly kept them balanced and level-headed as much as she could.

Mo was recruited his Junior year and decided to attend a Division 1 College on a full athletic scholarship in the D.C, Maryland, Virginia (DMV) area. All of Mo's hard work paid off nicely. His parents worked hard to keep obstacles out of his way and to keep him clean and healthy to earn a scholarship for his athletic ability. Mo made his parents and siblings proud. His parents were particularly pleased to not have to pay a third tuition while the second kid was still in school. They loved Mo for this!

Mo's sister was the oldest, equally as athletic as Mo, and was already in college when they met Mo. She ran track, the 400 (1 full lap around the track) and 400-meter hurdles (1 full lap around the track jumping over meticulously placed obstacles). She received some scholarship money to run but not a full scholarship. Mo's brother was an athlete as well and was two years older than Mo. He played basketball at their high school and was extremely smart. He wasn't offered a basketball scholarship but received several smaller academic scholarships and grants to help defray the cost of college.

16

Brandon and Racquel were not athletically endowed. Their favorite sports were Kickball and Dodgeball. They destroyed opponents in both games. Racquel was particularly fond of a good game of Kickball. She was not a sprinter but fast enough to rarely get out. She was known for kicking a line drive so hard that some kids' lips were busted in their attempts to bend over and snatch up the speeding ball. (This happened twice but in Racquel's mind, it happened regularly). Racquel ran her fastest to first base and sometimes glanced out to the left to see whether anyone intercepted the ball. She then continued to second base. She loved kickball and that was her sport.

Brandon loved a good game of Dodgeball. He was relentless in trying to destroy the heads, bodies, legs or vital organs of his opponents. He especially liked to throw the ball at the feet of someone running across the gym so that they would get entangled, fall to their knees and nearly cry from the pain. Head shots were especially fun and funny to Brandon. He was often a captain and he always picked Racquel to be on his team, so she was spared the torture of playing against him. On those rare occasions when she was his opponent, she feared for her life! Brandon would point to her, nod his head, and give her a joker like smile before he beamed the ball at her. "Just cruel!", Racquel thought, when the tables were turned, and she was dodging from him.

Nonetheless, that was about as far as either one of them ventured into the sports realm. They were so busy laughing and playing, that they often received lower grades in key classes. Racquel was a B sometimes C student. Brandon was a C sometimes D or occasionally a B student. Brandon's Mom wanted him to go to college and not sit around her house after graduation. Brandon was accepted to a couple of small colleges out in Ohio, Wisconsin and Florida. He was also accepted to their County Community College which he and his Mom agreed would be best. Ohio and Wisconsin were too cold and Florida might be too much fun & sun, and not enough college.

Racquel was accepted to and attended a university in the central part of Delaware. The day she received the acceptance, she literally jumped up and down. She could not believe it. She was so happy, she sprinted down the stairs to tell her mom and dad. She sent a text to Brandon and Mo and called Kelly to tell them she got in. Such a huge burden was lifted that day. Racquel knew that she was heading to college, like her parents before her, and like her three best friends. They all were heading to college and in a few short years with their Baccalaureate degrees in hand, they would become powerful alumni of their respective institutions. They were doing big things!

# CHAPTER THREE

THEIR HIGH SCHOOL GRADUATION was held at the football stadium on a beautiful, hot and humid day in mid-June. It was not a good hair day. The sky was blue and there were giant cumulus clouds as far as the eye could see. Racquel looked up at the bright, beautiful sky and thought some of the clouds resembled the opening scene of the Simpsons. The gates of the stadium opened at 5 pm for proud parents, God parents, guardians, aunts, uncles, brothers, sisters, cousins and friends to file in to support their young graduates.

At 5:50 pm, the soon to be graduates started to march in to the sounds of "Pomp and Circumstance" at a speed that would have the graduating class of 220 in their designated seats for a 6:05 pm ceremony start. None of the four of them were able to sit together because of their last names. Brandon talked to the Senior Class Advisor, Mrs. Stokes, during practice about letting friends sit together instead of by last name because it was their last big hoorah together. The Class Advisor simply told him, "No! not gonna happen! Now get back in line, and in alphabetical order BRANDON!" Mrs. Stokes put so much emphasis on his name that everyone on the field turned their attention toward them. Poor Brandon looked insulted and dejected.

Racquel's, Kelly's, Brandon's and Mo's family tried to sit together as much as possible so that they would have a huge crowd of people cheering for each one of them. The objective was to have

19

the loudest cheering section in the stadium. Brandon's mom, sister, grandparents and a couple of uncles, wives and girlfriends showed up to support Brandon. Kelly's mom, dad, three younger brothers, godmother and her husband, and a couple of single aunts showed up to support Kelly. Mo's doting mom, dad, older sister and fiancé, older brother, and a large posse of aunts, uncles and cousins showed up to support Mo. Racquel's Mom, Dad, and three siblings godfather, were there as well, along with her single godfather, favorite married aunt and uncle and their children; her two cousins. They all sat in the same section of the stands near to each other.

One of Kelly's aunts leaned in to ask, "Now, what's Brandon's last name? She wanted to be ready to cheer for each one of Kelly's best friends. All the families made sure that they had the last names of each of the four best friends and they cheered embarrassingly for each one of them.

Kelly H. (don't ask her about her middle name) Cook

Brandon Lamar Freeman

Morton Thomas Goodwin

Racquel Amani Wilson

Their families showed up and showed their butts in cheering for them, despite the requests to "please hold all applause …". Their families thumbed their noses at that request and did their own thing, as did many other families that day.

After sitting through a litany of boring speeches, corny administrators and what they perceived the future held for this graduating class, and encouragement to "seize the day", it was finally over!! Graduation caps with both inspiring and ridiculously dumb sayings were tossed high in the air towards the bright, beautiful, blue sky.

A tremendous number of pictures were taken. It was as if they had a shot list.

- Racquel and Mo's parents,
- Mo and Racquel' parents,
- Kelly and Racquel flanked by their parents,
- Brandon and everyone's parents
- Mo, Kelly, Brandon, and Racquel all together,
- Mo, Kelly, Brandon and Racquel with everyone's brothers and sisters,
- Racquel and Mo,
- Brandon and Racquel,
- Kelly, Racquel and just their moms,
- Mo and his Dad,
- Kelly and her aunts,
- Mo and his uncles,
- Brandon and his grandparents and on and on.

They stood at the stadium for close to an hour taking pictures. Eventually, everyone went their separate ways to enjoy dinner with their respective families. Racquel did not understand what the big fuss over high school graduation was about. They all were headed to college and those graduations would be bigger than this one. Nonetheless, it was special to Racquel that she had made such good friends since Kindergarten and it was important to her that they all remained friends throughout their college years.

Racquel envisioned the four of them opening a business together utilizing all their talents. Just the four of them, FOREVER!

# La Onque Chavette

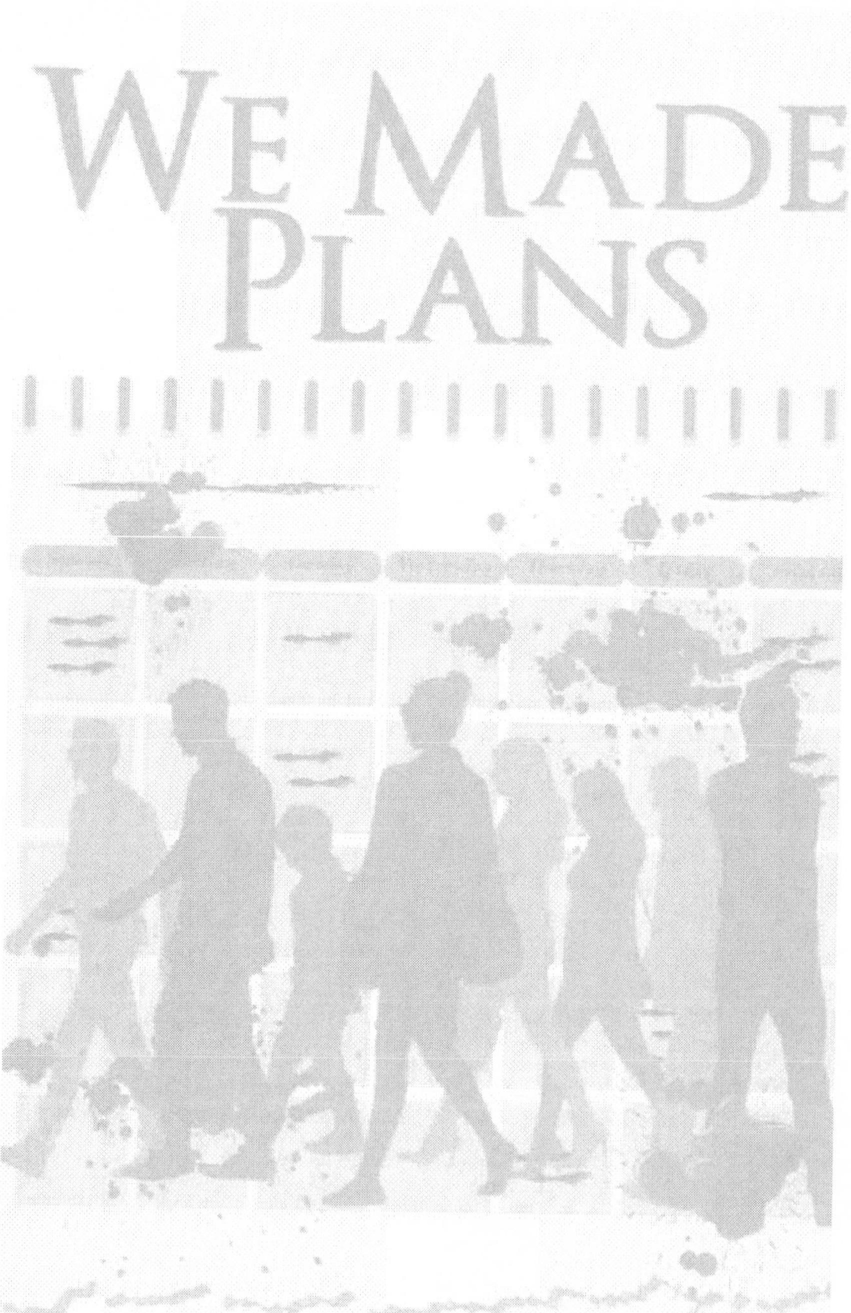
WE MADE PLANS

# CHAPTER FOUR

**G**ETTING SETTLED INTO THE COLLEGE CAMPUS life was tricky. Racquel's parents, her godmother, who was divorced from her godfather who attended the graduation, came with her new husband, and Racquel's youngest brother all helped move her into college that last weekend in August for freshman orientation. They helped her unpack, they all said prayer and then her mom wrote on the pad outside of her door, "DON'T WASTE MY MONEY!". They left and Racquel didn't see them again until Thanksgiving break.

So much happened those first few months. Someone stole Racquel's favorite designer wristlet at one of the first parties she attended with the upper classmen. Older junior and senior guys tried to prey on every Freshman girl with the right proportion of a waist and butt/thighs. It was flattering to Racquel at first but quickly became a little annoying. "My parents didn't raise no fool", Racquel thought to herself and then thought that she was starting to sound a little like Kelly. But it was true!

Racquel's parents were both college graduates. In fact, Racquel's mom followed her Dad to campus a year after he arrived. He helped her complete the application and welcomed her with open arms. After being on campus herself for a couple of weeks, Racquel was pretty sure that wasn't the only way her Dad welcomed her

Mom to campus. Anyway, graduation, marriage, and three kids later, there was Racquel.

Her parents always spoke openly with her, especially her Mom. They often had uncomfortably candid conversations for a mother and daughter, but she tried to educate Racquel on many things the textbooks didn't cover. She never wanted anyone to take advantage of Racquel, mistreat her or mistake her for somebody's fool. Both parents instilled in her that she was a Child of God and a representative of their family name. That's why Racquel and Kelly got along so well. They had similar backgrounds, but Kelly was more strict in the application of her parent's instructions. She took them seriously and always wanted to honor her mother and father. Racquel straddled the fence and liked to laugh and play far more. Racquel found humor in almost everything.

However, the overly aggressive, rather vulgar, college guys were not funny to Racquel. They tried relentlessly to invade her personal space. She had to let them know quickly that she wasn't the one to be played with. If she didn't, she would've garnered a reputation that she did not want the burden of carrying for the next few years in the unforgiving society she lived in.

At the freshman orientation weekend, Racquel met Candice Alicia Thomas (Cat for short) and Sydney Marie Ellison, soon to be known around campus as Dancing Sydney. People had to distinguish her from a couple of other Sydneys on campus, particularly Fat Sydney. Candice and Sydney were cool, liked to have fun, and occasionally drank but did not get pissy drunk. Candice and Sydney would become Racquel's new best friends for the next four years. They had Racquel's back and she had theirs.

# La Onque Chavette

Candice was from North Carolina but didn't have an accent because her parents were from New Jersey and refused to let her mispronounce words in a "southern drawl". They couldn't stand it and often corrected her harshly to speak the way they spoke. Candice was cute, short, had big brown eyes that her parents had to have adored, and medium length hair. She often wore it in longer braids because it was just easier to deal with daily as opposed to her own natural hair. She was your typical short and feisty friend who one would eventually have to save from a beat down from someone twice her size because she just talked so much trash.

Despite the trash talking flaw, Candice was super smart and in college specifically to major in biomedical engineering. She was a science whiz who eagerly helped Racquel through Spring semester Biology II. After that class, Racquel stopped taking science courses that weren't required for graduation. Candice received A's and B's in most of the classes her freshman year except for one. She was devastated when she received her first C. Sydney and Racquel had to console her and talk her down from going to curse the professor out for giving her a C+ instead of a B. She was infuriated!

Candice was funny to Racquel because she was focused, pragmatic and smart but so feisty and difficult to deal with. She thrived on confrontation. She was a complex personality type that Racquel had not encountered in her entire life.

Sydney was reasonably smart and a dance major. She was tall, long with shapely dancer's legs and an almost perfect butt, as a result of years of dance training from the age of four. Her feet were not so perfect, but most people didn't see her feet and most guys who had access to view those toes weren't really interested in her feet anyway. Sydney attracted most of the attention from the aggressive, vulgar upper classmen. Racquel often thought the attention she received was the residual from hanging out with Sydney. She was beautiful, charming like Mo, had a contagious laugh like Brandon and was always the life of the party. People often sent messages to Sydney to find out where the parties were. She regularly had the answers because she was always invited or made aware of all things social.

Neither Sydney nor Candice were devout Christians like Kelly, but they knew some typical bible verses and sometimes referred to them. The usual verses that most Christian children learned in Sunday school and church services such as,

> *"In the beginning God created the heaven and earth" Genesis1:1 KJV*

> *"For God so loved the world, that he gave his only begotten Son, that whoever believeth in him should not perish, but have everlasting life" John 3:16 KJV*

> *"The Lord is my Shepherd; I shall not want..." Psalms 23:1 KJV*

Shortly after reciting any of these three famous biblical quotes, the conversation would deteriorate to a story laced with curse words and the mother of all profanities, FUCK. Racquel often pointed this contradiction out to them that, for example, the bible says,

> *"Out of the same mouth proceedeth blessing and cursing. My brethren, these things ought not so to be" James 3:10 KJV.*

Racquel would change brethren to "sisters" but they didn't pay any mind to what she was saying, except to point out that they were pretty sure the bible did not state "sisters". Racquel would roll her eyes at them and say, "Semantics! Y'all are going to Hell!"

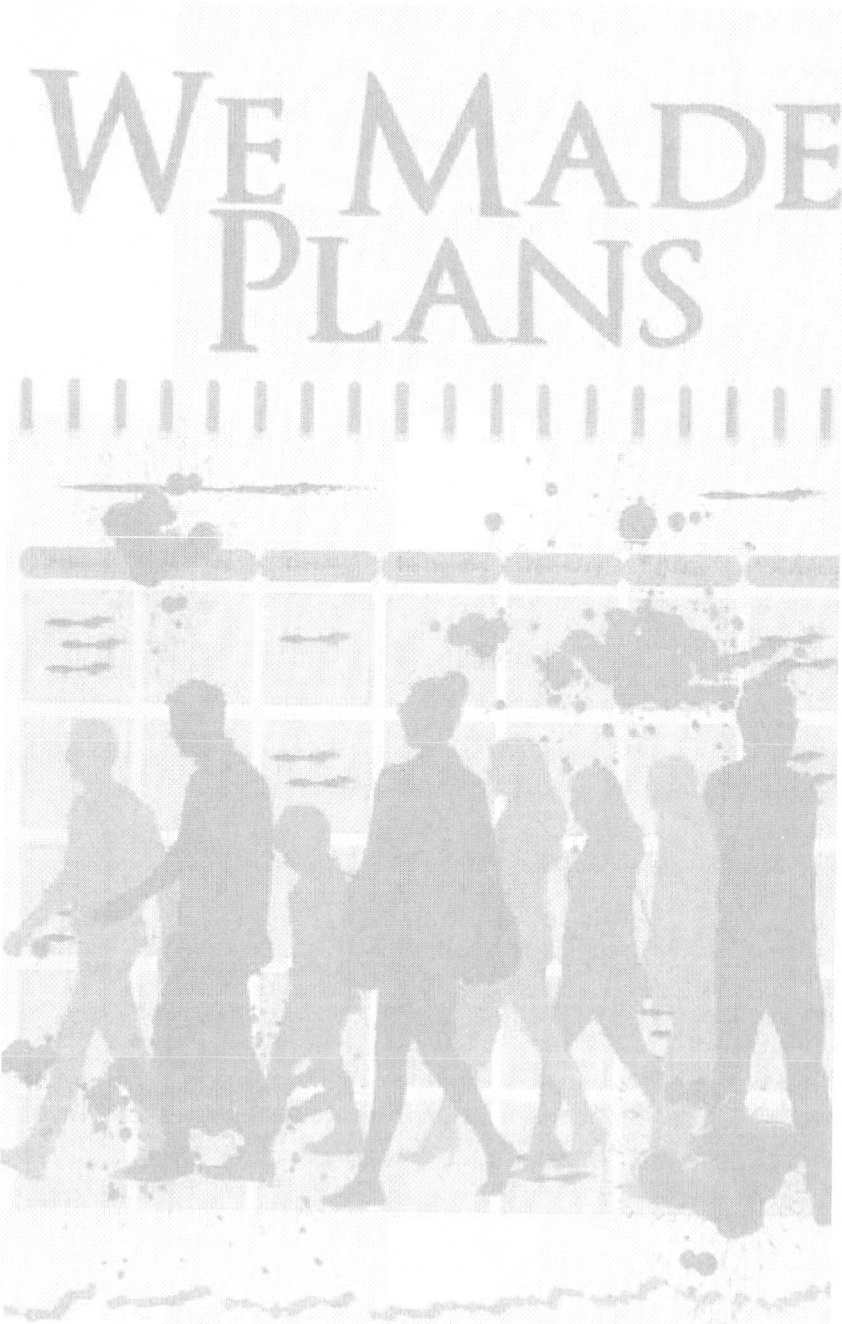
We Made
Plans

# CHAPTER FIVE

I**T AS CHRISTMAS BREAK** and Racquel couldn't wait to see her parents, her siblings, Brandon, Mo, and Kelly. Racquel hugged everyone so hard and for what seemed like two minutes each. She enveloped every second of the embrace just thankful to be in their presence. They were her peace and the balance she needed. Family was everything to Racquel.

Racquel, Brandon, Kelly and Mo went to their local Delaware mall to do some Christmas shopping for family. After peaking into a few overpriced stores, they ended up at the food court and talked for hours catching up over latte's, Thai food, pizza, wings, chicken fingers, and deli sandwiches. They each talked about their wacked college experiences, what they were majoring in and what they thought they might change their majors to. The four of them talked about the creepy guys and girls, their amazing and brilliant professors and politics for hours. Their conversation returned to what they were buying their families for Christmas but then quickly drifted back to college life and visiting each other's campus in the Spring.

Kelly, little Miss Organized, took control of that task and set three weekends for them to visit each other on campus. She had to coordinate around Mo's sports schedule and everyone's finals week, but she successfully mapped it out.  They made plans to meet up.

After about 2 hours of sitting, eating and talking, they took off to resume their Christmas shopping for family.

# CHAPTER SIX

**M**ID SPRING OF THE SECOND SEMESTER of their freshman year, they visited Mo's campus. Kelly coordinated with Mo so that their visit corresponded with his college's spring football game. Mo was very popular on campus and naturally so. He was still good looking and charming. His face was even more chiseled. His daily, grueling workouts caused every muscle in his body to be boldly defined and his dreadlocks were even further down his back than when Racquel saw him for Christmas. This was the best Racquel had seen Mo look in their entire lifetime together (4 years). Racquel finally looked at Mo and saw him.

"I don't remember Mo looking this good during Christmas." Racquel thought to herself . "Why does he look so good now?" she wondered. Racquel took a long, quiet, deep breath and thought to herself, "And why does he smell so good?" This was not the Mo from high school or Christmas for that matter. Something was up.

Mo introduced Racquel, Kelly and Brandon to lots of new teammates, some equally as good looking, built and charming as Mo. He also introduced them to a few groupies. He called them "friends" but Racquel and Kelly knew the type and they determined they should be called GROUPIES. They were there strictly to cheer them on and fulfill whatever other desires they had. Some hoped to latch on long enough to marry and hoped even more to get a big pay day from such impressive specimens of athletes. Kelly and Racquel were cordial but as soon as the four of them were alone again, Mo got an earful. To which he snatched both of them up, squeezed them ridiculously hard, kissed their heads and thanked them for being real friends. Kelly told him to shut up before he made her cry. For that comment, she received a second kiss on the forehead.

Brandon had no problems with Mo's friends, especially the groupies. They laughed at everything he said. Brandon was hilarious and always kept the group in stitches. A party just wasn't a party if Brandon wasn't there. He and Mo were like brothers by this point. They always consulted with and confided in each other. Of course, Brandon had questions about certain "friends/groupies" at the end of the night.

A couple of weeks later, it was Racquel's turn to host the second leg of their campus tour. Brandon came a day earlier than Kelly and Mo because his classes were done early on Thursday afternoon. Racquel took Brandon to the student center to meet some friends and then to the dining hall for lunch. There they met up with Candice and Sydney. Brandon seemed to have taken one look at Candice and fell in love instantly. He introduced himself and everything about Brandon changed that day. His voice was even deeper. Racquel snapped her head around, frowned, and raised her eyebrows all at once to see where the deeper voice was coming from because it didn't sound at all like Brandon. His posture was better. He was a little more serious than the jokester he usually was. Candice was so giggly and silly, not at all confrontational. Racquel couldn't believe what she was witnessing and thought to herself, "what the hell?" It resembled puppy love at first sight.

That night Brandon grilled Racquel about all things Candice.

La Onque Chavette

He even asked Racquel why she didn't tell him more about Candice during the Christmas break.  He said that Candice was his "kind of woman" and that Racquel was holding out on him.  Racquel laughed and reminded him that she didn't befriend Candice with him in mind and added that she didn't know what kind of woman he liked anyway.  Needless to say, Brandon and Candice were hooked on each other from the moment they met, and it was an extremely looooooong weekend.

Mo and Kelly arrived the next day and they had a great time but it was never just the four of them like the few weeks prior when they visited Mo.  They had a fifth wheel now and her name was Candice Alicia Thomas, but it was sort of ok.

Mo, true to his charming nature, made lots of friends on Racquel's campus.  He even talked to other athletes and shared social media information.  He clearly liked the way Sydney looked but he did not engage in prolonged conversations.  He kept a modest distance.  Sydney didn't spend as much time with them that weekend but enough for it to be a great and memorable weekend for them all.

Later, they all made plans to see each other during the summer and go out to Kelly's campus in NY just before they went home for Christmas break.  Christmas in NY seemed like what movies were made of.  They were, indeed, exactly what many movies were made of.  So, that's what they did.  They made plans to meet up.

Brandon took two summer classes and made trips between each session to visit Candice in North Carolina.  Candice's parents really liked him, and he was happy about that.  Brandon came out to visit Racquel, Candice and Sydney, or just Candice really, during the first weekend back their sophomore year of college.  He also came out to a couple of additional weekends and Homecoming. He was addicted to Candice and she was addicted to him. Racquel was amazed that two of her good friends, from two different worlds, found themselves so in love. She was, however, also deeply concerned that a break-up between the two of them would force her to choose between friends and she didn't want to deal with that burden. They assured Racquel that if that happened, they would not try to pit her against the other. Promises, Promises.

# CHAPTER SEVEN

**I**T WAS ABOUT A FULL WEEK BEFORE CHRISTMAS and everyone was finishing up classes and finals and preparing to meet up shortly in NY to visit Kelly's campus. Of course, when you go to school in NY, NY is the campus. At least that's what all your non-native NY friends think. They weren't interested in the beautiful historic buildings or the mature, tree lined paths to get to them. They didn't care about the deep history of Kelly's Ivy league University or who was the first this or that to attend and graduate. They weren't concerned about the intricate details because the reality was that they were only out there to see the city, New York City. The places they saw in movies and heard of from other friends who lived in or frequented NY was what they were anxious to experience.

Kelly's campus was beautiful but her dorm room was nothing spectacular. They were there for about 90 minutes catching up, meeting a couple of her friends and touring the campus. Then it was time to see the real stuff. NYC baby!!!

Although they all grew up in Delaware, they never ventured out to New York except for a class trip to the Statue of Liberty in the second grade. New York is experienced differently as a second grader with your teacher and someone's overweight, hippy Mom chaperoning as opposed to your second year of college with good friends, new-found freedoms and perspectives.

They dropped all their bags off in Kelly's dorm room. They weren't lugging all that stuff around the city all day. They were anxious to get to Manhattan and see the sites. Oh yes, and Candice was with them or, technically, with Brandon. They visited the Rockefeller Center to see and take pictures in front of the tree. Of course, Brandon and Racquel jumped at the opportunity to take pictures with the giant cartoon characters who, short of harassed them for a tip after taking the picture.

They looked at and passed by the ice-skating rink but didn't try it out. God forbid someone twists an ankle, tears an ACL or breaks a leg. No time for that! They made plans for the day and dealing with a NY hospital emergency room was NOT in their plans.

They stopped to gaze at and admire the skaters who were moving so smoothly and effortlessly around the rink. Some looked as if they were professional ice skaters. Yet others steadied themselves with their feet hip width apart, butts protruding, arms out, hoping to take the next step forward without falling over. Amateurs and beginners lined the wall of the rink close enough to grab it and hold on for dear life should they start to fall.

From Rockefeller Center they made their way through the packed, busy streets over to Macy's Herald Square. They window shopped, took silly pictures to post on social media and stood in line to take pictures with Santa Clause for about ten minutes. They then decided that they were too old for that, that the line was too long, and it would waste too much time for a one-day visit to NY.

They ventured a couple of blocks over to Madison Square

Garden. Mo refused to go to NY and not visit "The Garden". There was no way they were heading back to Kelly's campus without making that stop. Mo needed the perfect picture to send to his brother and doting Mom. So, he stood with his arms stretched out wide, like he was king of the world, had a huge smile on his face and said ready. But it's hard to capture that picture without strangers in it. NY streets are busy and ruthless.

They had to try to take the picture 4 different times and yell at him from the edge of the street, "OK NOW!" And hope that New Yorkers would be kind enough to avoid walking into the picture, but they didn't give two shits about Mo's picture. Mo kept running over to look at the phone and then decided they were done and said, "Thanks, send me the pics."

Racquel, Brandon, Kelly, Mo and Candice visited lots of street vendors and picked up cute, useless Christmas gifts for their families. Hat and scarf sets were best sellers!! You get a set! And you get a set! And you get a set! Five people scratched off their Christmas lists. Mo even purchased a CD to help one of the street vendors. Brandon and Candice tried to pull him away and keep it moving but he wanted to help. Kelly and Racquel later questioned whether there was really music on the CD and then teased him about where he was going to find a CD player to play his new music-less CD. Kelly said, "Mo, you bought the CD for $5 and you don't even have a car with a CD player in it, what sense does that make?"

Mo looked at Kelly, paused as if he wanted to say ten foul mouthed things to her, pointed at her and then simply said, "don't worry about my CD little girl!" Kelly laughed and slapped his hand away from her face. "I'm not a little girl!", she said and walked away. Mo waited for her to get far enough away so she was just out of range and then pretended to give her a swift kick in the butt.

39

# We Made Plans

Racquel said to Mo, "You know Kelly won't "turn the other cheek" if you kick her in the butt, no pun intended" and burst into laughter. Kelly whipped around and in a high-pitched voice said, "Mo! did you just try to kick me?" Mo moved in quickly and grabbed her so that her arms were pressed to her sides and said, "No Kelly, we're in NY, we gotta stick together, now stop acting up!"

Brandon and Candice moved through the city constantly holding hands or walking with their arms around each other. Occasionally, Candice would jump on his back to get a piggyback ride for half a block before she slid off and decided to walk like a normal person. They stopped at one of the Sabrett hotdog vendor carts on the street. The ones where you wonder how they wash their hands or where they put their cart when they must use the bathroom. You wonder about all types of hygiene issues related to an outdoor, pushcart, hotdog vendor, then say to yourself, "oh well, God made dirt and dirt don't hurt" and proceed to eat those dirty dogs.

Everyone paid for their own hotdogs except Brandon. He paid for Candice's food and drink as well. He was really trying to impress Candice. Racquel purchased two hotdogs with mustard and sweet relish and bottled water. Mo bought 3 chili cheese dogs, two cans of grape soda and a bag of chips and wolfed it down remarkably fast. Kelly bought one hotdog with sauerkraut and mustard and an orange soda. They each forgot to get napkins and the vendor only gave Mo three napkins, so they were pretty much a mess, walking, talking and eating the best, dirtiest, sloppiest hotdogs ever.

They took group selfies. They didn't trust strangers to hold their phones to take full body pictures of the five of them. So, they took mostly fathead shots with the five of them squeezed into the screen with bright eyes, goofy smiles and no cares in the world.

40

"We in NYC!!!!!!." They all said with goofy smiles and snapped the picture which was shared to all of their phones, posted to social media in less than 1 minute and labeled **#ChristmasinNYbaby**" Racquel really wanted a picture of just her, Brandon, Mo and Kelly, the long-time friends, since kindergarten and high school but she didn't want to offend Brandon and Candice and spoil the fun they were having.

They had such an extraordinary time in NY that they made plans to visit again the next Christmas and to make it a yearly tradition. FOREVER!

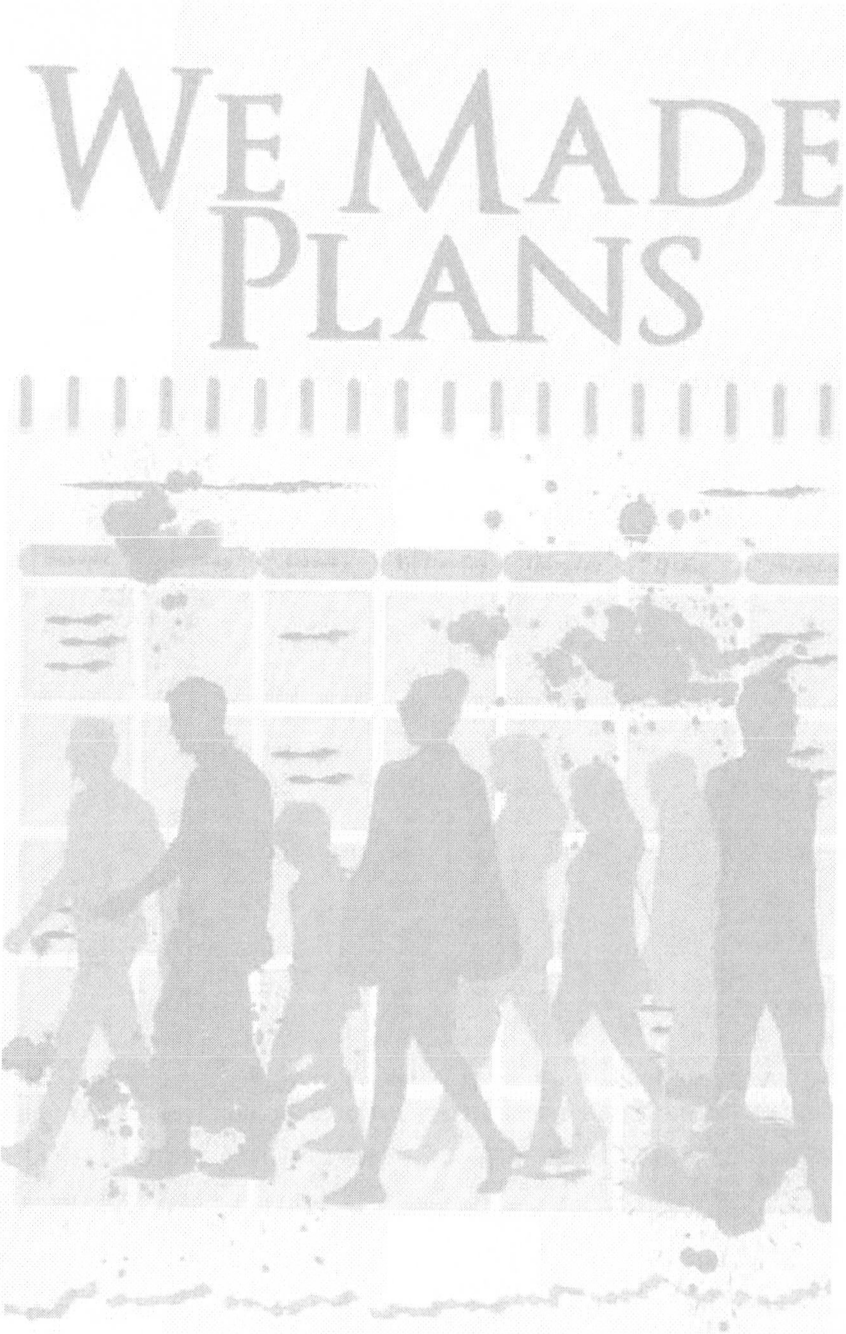
WE MADE
PLANS

# CHAPTER EIGHT

**R**ACQUEL DIDN'T THINK when they left for college that she would see so much of Brandon, but there he was. Racquel thought it was good that he didn't reside on campus with them because Candice was able to focus on her incredibly, complicated, mind boggling (to Racquel anyway) biomedical engineering courses. Candice was still doing well in her classes and officially declared it as her major. She was going to graduate with a degree that would make her parents proud!

However, that previous Christmas when they were all enjoying New York, Brandon quietly met the deadline to apply for admission to Racquel's university. He would be finishing up his second year of community college that Spring and decided that he wanted to be on campus with Candice. Racquel couldn't say that he wanted to be on campus with her because she knew the ONLY reason he applied to her university was because of Candice and their ongoing love affair.

Overall, Racquel was thrilled that Brandon was happy, and Candice was a good friend. There was no indication of a breakup anytime soon, so life was easy. Brandon was accepted to Racquel's university and he was going to major in Logistics and Supply Chain Management. When he told Racquel about the salary potential, she thought about switching her major. When Racquel thought about Brandon and Candice's combined earning potential if they were to get married, she asked them to adopt her.

Fall semester of their Junior year, Candice, Sydney and Racquel were able to get into the luxury apartments in the heart of the campus, centrally located near everything that was anything. They were near the sports complex that housed the basketball arena, near the Student Center and the endless number of fast food restaurants it housed. The apartments were near two of the major buildings that offered the 200-person freshman seminars and other core prerequisite courses. They were near one of the buildings that housed the Deans, Directors of Programs of Study, and select professors which was great for visiting during their office hours. It was a perfect location!

The luxury apartment was in a 10-story building that overlooked the sports complex on one side, the small man-made lake and young, tree lined walking trail on another side. They offered single bedroom apartments to graduate students only and three, four, and five-bedroom combination apartments to undergraduate juniors and seniors.

Racquel, Candice and Sydney stayed in a three bedroom, each with its own attached bathroom (princess suites), a kitchen with modern cabinets, granite countertops and island, wood laminate flooring for easy cleanup (college life gets messy) and a comfortable size living room. The living room area was furnished with a black leather couch, two end tables, a coffee table, one table lamp, accent chair, and a wall mount sturdy enough to accommodate a 65-inch tv. Their windows spanned from the floorboards to the ceiling and came with room darkening curtains atop sheer curtains. Each bedroom had a small, walk-in closet, a full-size bed, a dresser drawer and a desk. They were, after all, still in college. A desk was mandatory.

Brandon was a transfer and not yet eligible to participate in the lottery for the luxury apartments. He stayed in a dorm about a half mile away with another transfer from Colorado. Brandon wondered why a college student would move from a state that offered legal recreational marijuana to a state that did not. His roommate was a special character and clearly did not care that his new state didn't endorse recreational marijuana use.

Brandon's room was small, appeared to be made from cinder blocks and painted a dismal off white. It contained the standard extra-long twin bed, desk, dresser drawer, and small closet. Absolutely nothing spectacular. He shared a bathroom with four stalls and four individual showers with the residents of the other 5 rooms on the third floor.

Brandon was ok with the set up, but Candice was not. Therefore, Brandon often stayed in their apartment. It was ok with Racquel as long as he didn't go more than two weeks without making all of them a Saturday morning breakfast which included bacon, cheese-eggs, pancakes and orange juice or some combination of bacon, eggs, and waffles etc. Whatever it was, it had to have bacon and eggs.

Candice had to make serious adjustments to having Brandon on campus regularly and balancing her increasingly difficult 300/400 level courses for her major. Halfway through the fall semester, Candice nearly failed her midterm exam in one of her classes. She and Brandon had a sit-down which was supposed to result in more individual study time and less snuggle time. That lasted for less than 10 days. They decided to combine study time so that they were in each other's presence but, yet, studying.  This task was sometimes moved to the library instead of Candice's cozy room to ensure real study time.

# CHAPTER NINE

O**VER IN NEW YORK,** Kelly seemed to be getting quite comfortable with a senior on campus. His name was Ezekiel. It truly figures that she would be interested in a man with such a biblical name as Ezekiel. She was probably more attracted to his name than him at first meeting. Some of his friends called him Zeke but he always introduced himself as Ezekiel. He was a junior and he and his Dad were proud of their family name. "There was no doubt in his mind that he would beget a son to whom he and his father's name would be given, and that son would become the third generation of Ezekiel Samuel Ellington's." Raquel thought to herself in her interpretation of a biblical voice.

Ezekiel was taller than Kelly just enough for her to wear a modest 3-inch heel and still look up at him when they were dressed up. He was a budding law school student and just finished taking his Law School Admission Test (LSAT) for the last time. He was applying to several law schools all over the country and Kelly was aware that he may leave to go somewhere non conducive to a flourishing relationship. Yet, they continued the dating and courting path. Zeke was a gentleman, polite, respectable, opened car doors, held regular doors, believed in the man as the head of the household, and had a strong faith. He clearly had a relationship with God. He seemed to be one of the people the biblical verse referred to, when it stated, "the prayers of the righteous availeth much". He was that guy! It also helped that he was cute, had a nice body and took good care of his "temple". Perfect for Kelly!

Kelly decided to major in Public Health and wanted to pursue her Master of Public Health (MPH) upon graduation. She also declared her major and was working toward finishing up the requirements a semester earlier than the full four years. Kelly contemplated Law School as Zeke was always in her ear discussing hot topics and their legal effect on society. They would sit for hours discussing how her interest in Public health could be enhanced by adding a Juris Doctorate (JD) and passing the Bar exam. He advised that she could move her career in different directions and work in higher levels of government and business if she pursued an interest in Law. He was very persuasive when he spoke. He presented as knowledgeable on diverse topics. Again, when Racquel thought of the combined earning potential for Zeke and Kelly as lawyers, she wanted them to adopt her.

Racquel's friends were doing well. They had so much potential in so many aspects of their lives and she was happy for them. Sydney, however, had a hard time working off the tales of her freshman year antics. She had settled down a little bit but still enjoyed having an extraordinary amount of fun. She didn't think girls should settle down so young. She thought that having a steady boyfriend over a few years in college was ridiculous and that those types of girls were missing out on life. She didn't keep a boyfriend for more than a semester, if she had someone she called a boyfriend at all. Sydney sometimes had random guys over on a Friday night who awoke hungry and trying to partake in Brandon's Saturday morning breakfast. They had a sit-down with Sydney and told her that sharing their breakfast with her random male friends wasn't going to work. Bacon cost too much and tasted too good to share like that. Eventually, her randoms would be hustled out, past the kitchen and out the door, all while sniffing and marveling at the remarkable breakfast they would NOT partake in.

We Made Plans

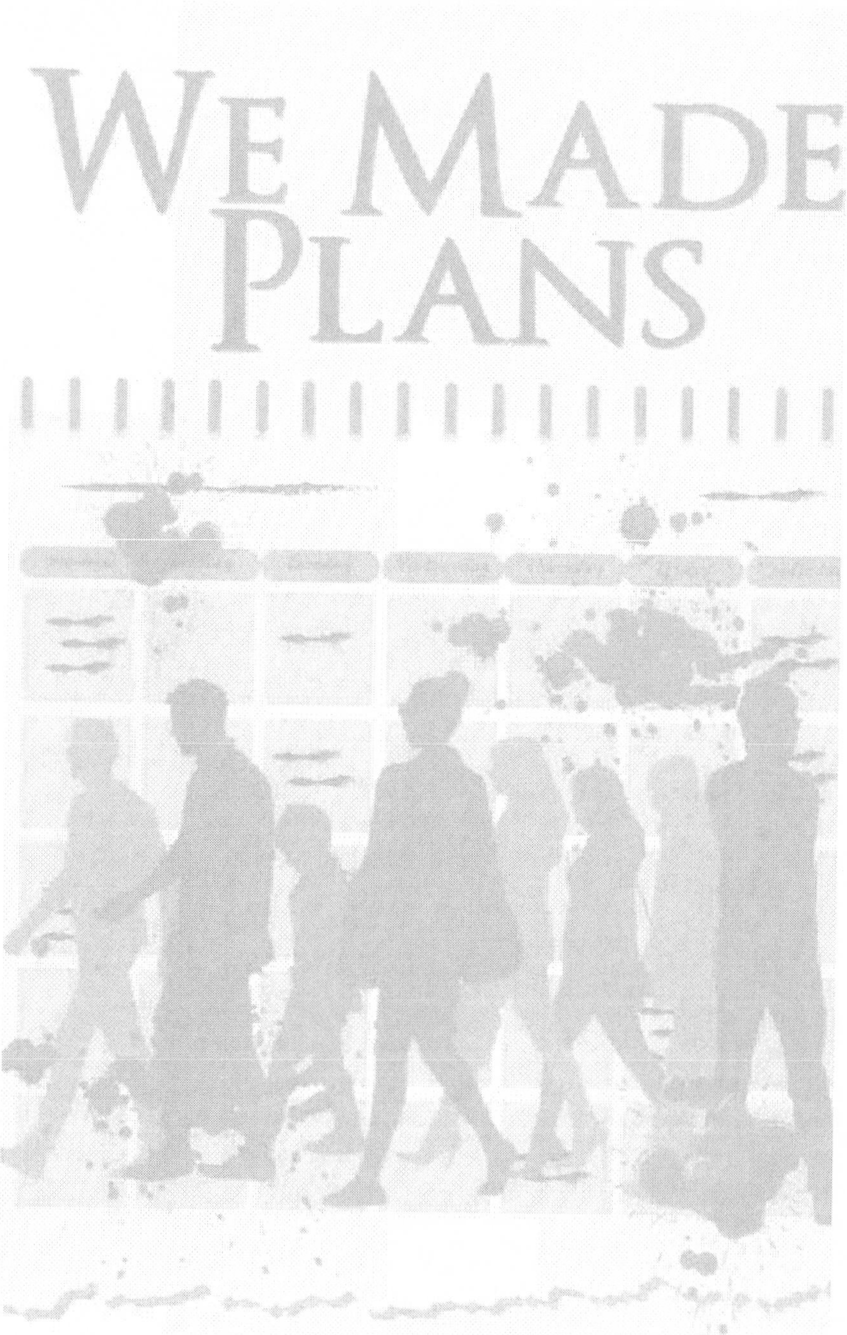

# CHAPTER TEN

**M**O WAS STARTING THE FALL of their junior year and wanted everyone to come out for homecoming to see him play. Kelly and Zeke drove to Racquel in a huge SUV Zeke's Dad rented. Then Zeke, Kelly, Brandon, Candice, Sydney and Racquel all piled in comfortably and drove to see Mo for Homecoming.

The atmosphere was exciting, the drumline was good, and they didn't have to pay for tickets to get in. Mo played a monster game. Racquel almost lost her voice cheering for him. It was a perfect day to be in the stands.

Mo tried to grill Zeke in a big brotherly kind of way but there was nothing wrong with Zeke. He was perfect for Kelly and presented very well. Mo mentioned to Sydney how long it had been since he'd seen her and that she looked good. He introduced them to a few of his teammates, some of whom, they met the last time they were there.

When they arrived back at Mo's apartment that he shared with 3 other teammates, there was a celebration going on because of the win, homecoming, and just because. His 800 square foot apartment was crowded and packed tight from wall to wall. It was hot and uncomfortable. The usual groupies were there along with a few new ones, teammates and tons of NARPS (non-athletic regular persons) wanting to celebrate at what appeared to be the hottest spot on campus, figuratively and literally. Mo moved all of them to his room and locked the door behind him. His room was amazingly clean. He told them they could sit on his bed and elsewhere. He grabbed some clothes, ran into the bathroom, took a quick shower and emerged fully clothed, lotioned and spritzed with a light cologne that smelled delightfully inviting.

Racquel was a little annoyed that he emerged fully clothed, but it would have been inappropriate for him to come out with just a towel on in front of everyone, showing off his chiseled body, although that's what she really wanted to see. He did, at least, put on a muscle shirt that fit enough to show off shoulders, biceps and abs. Racquel thought she should have been happy with that.

They all partied at Mo's apartment for a few hours and then headed out to one of the homecoming events. One of Mo's teammates was drooling behind Sydney all night. Everyone seemed to be coupled up so Mo and Racquel hung out and talked about the game, professional league prospects, what he was majoring in and how he was doing in school. They talked about his grades and life after college if it didn't involve a professional league. They talked about ex-girlfriends and ex-boyfriends, his teammates and Brandon's wacky, weed smoking roommate. They talked about Brandon and Candice and how perfect Zeke and Kelly seemed together. Mo also mentioned that his teammate was a good guy and how he didn't want Sydney playing with his head. Racquel frowned and told Mo that Sydney was a good person and she didn't want his roommate trying to use her either.

To avoid another heated debate that Mo and Racquel often got into over everything, they changed the subject to talk about her.

52

Mo asked numerous questions that night. Racquel felt like she was on trial, but she was flattered that he was sincerely interested in what was going on with her in the midst of all that he had going on in his life.

# CHAPTER ELEVEN

**T**HE END OF YET ANOTHER SEMESTER had come and gone, and they made plans to meet up in NY. There was the looming threat that Mo wasn't going to be able to make it if his team went to a bowl game. Racquel really wanted Mo to go because he was so much fun. She knew Zeke and Kelly and Brandon and Candice were going. Sydney hadn't been yet and wasn't planning on attending. Racquel would have been a fifth wheel and felt like it. Unfortunately for Mo, but fortunately for them, Mo's team didn't go to a bowl game.

Mo was distraught about it because it was an important year for professional scouting. He vowed to make sure that his team made it to a bowl game the following year. He already planned to put in five years under his scholarship. He needed his team to become conference champions and make it to a bowl game. He said that's what he was going to work on and everything else was going to fall into place.

Racquel reminded Mo that's not how it works! "Seek ye first the Kingdom of God, and his righteousness, and all things will be added unto you, Matthew six something". Mo threw his head back and cracked up laughing. With watery eyes, from laughing so hard, he looked at Racquel smiled and said, "see, that's what I need, a praying woman". Then he said, "You're funny." Racquel was taken aback and wondered why her comment made him laugh so hard but his laugh was contagious, and she laughed at him laughing at her. "Whatever Mo!", Racquel said. She didn't pursue the comment about him "needing a praying woman". She just wondered how serious he was about that and thought that if he was really attracted to her, they would be in a relationship by now.

That Christmas Mo invited himself to Racquel's family's annual Christmas morning breakfast. He gave her parents a nice gift that he tricked her into recommending when they were shopping in New York by saying, "you think my mom and dad would like this? Would you buy it for your parents?" He also had Racquel sniff various perfumes until she was almost nauseous.

He bought, wrapped and gave Racquel the perfume that she thought she selected for his sister. She loved that perfume and was glad to have it but what a devious move. After her family opened gifts, Racquel said, "Ok Mo, I see how you do". She told her parents how he "chose" the gifts and they laughed and thought it was a great way to do it. Racquel's mom said, "that was ingenious Mo. Thanks for thinking of us sweetie" and gave him a hug and kiss.

Mo and Racquel never exchanged gifts before. None of the four of them exchanged gifts because they never had enough money to buy for their families and for each other. They just enjoyed shopping together in NY before heading home. Mo stayed over for half of Christmas Day and invited Racquel back to his house for Christmas dinner. The big thing on Christmas day at Racquel's house was breakfast so it was ok for her to leave for a little while for dinner.

# La Onque Chavette

When she asked Mo why he bought her a gift this year, he said because he had the money and he just wanted to get her something nice for always being a good friend and having his back. He said to her, "I know you pray for me, don't you" and laughed. To which she said, "why do you always laugh about my scripture quoting and prayer life?

Mo looked at her and with a serious, straight face, he said, "Your scripture quoting is a little off! How are you going to say Matthew six something? I need to know the EXACT chapter and verse, Bible Betty!" Racquel laughed at being called "Bible Betty" and lightly punched him in the stomach. Mo doubled over and laughed even harder. Then Mo said, "you're going to have to figure out those bible verses before we have kids, talking about Matthew six something", as he kept laughing. Racquel stopped laughing abruptly and said, "wait what? Kiiiidzzzz?"

Racquel tried to contain her excitement at the thought of a lifetime commitment and kids with Mo. He was great and his family was wonderful. His doting Mom loved her, and her parents loved Mo. Their kids would be unbelievably spoiled rotten by both sets of grandparents. They would have so many aunts, uncles and cousins. Family trips to Disney, The Caribbean, Italy and Africa! She imagined what their son would look like and if she would be as doting as Mo's mom was over him.

If they had a girl, would she have his almost hazel eyes. She would be so cute. He would probably spoil her rotten and not let any boys talk to her. And if her brother or brothers were older, then she could just forget it. How tall would their son be? Would he be somewhere in between their height? Oh Lord, what would she do if their son looked just like Mo! She would have to keep the girls away! "RACQUEL!" Mo yelled interrupting her train of thought

57

and laughing at her. Mo said, "yeaaaahh, you're thinking about the possibilities, you were seriously daydreaming, hahahaaaaaaaaa!"

"Shut up Mo and don't play with people's emotions like that" Racquel belted out and started to walk away. Mo grabbed her arm to pull her back and she snatched it away and kept walking for the stairs to the first floor. He grabbed her arm again, pulled her in to him saying, "I'm sorry Roc," and kissed her. She was astonished but did not resist.

# CHAPTER TWELVE

**A**FTER CHRISTMAS DAY THEIR JUNIOR YEAR, Mo and Racquel talked more often on the phone, texted regularly and met up, just the two of them, without their entourage of friends. He had small windows of time between practices and seasons, so they had to make the most of it. They talked about Florida for Spring break but didn't have enough money to go. They made plans to try to go during Spring break, Senior year. They still hadn't decided whether to tell their good friends what was going on between them.

Mo decided to major in criminal justice with a concentration in homeland security. Racquel said, "wow Mo, that's great!" He had already taken enough of those classes to declare it as his major. He really seemed to enjoy the coursework and was doing well in his classes. The Professors saw huge potential for him in this field and beyond football. They were very encouraging.

Mo also started to dominate in football and heard murmurs of professional league interest. There was even discussion of potential agents. It was an exciting time. Mo stayed busy, ate right, tried to stay healthy and out of trouble. He distanced himself from the groupies and really focused on the goals and plans he was making. Mo even started reading his bible regularly. He was laser focused.

# We Made Plans

Racquel was contemplating how quickly her college years were passing by. She thought to herself that graduation was creeping up rapidly. "I'm faced with the fact that I need to get a job before I graduate. But first I need to do an internship. But the priority is to apply for grad school which means I must take the test, so the priority is then the test?? Wait, what exactly am I doing?" Racquel rubbed her forehead in distress. "How do I prioritize all of this? "Will I even graduate this year?" Racquel stressfully pondered.

Needless to say, Racquel was uneasy and anxious as she began her senior year and a little lost about what to do next. Her world revolved around her friends and family her entire life and now it was getting real. Racquel knew that she would have to make a name for herself. She couldn't continue to hide behind the brilliance, talents and earning potential of her best friends. Besides, she had two great parents and no one was adopting her.

Racquel had about 12 credits of 300/400 level courses remaining that she had to take before graduation. She thought it best to split those up between the two semesters so that she wasn't overwhelmed. "I'll take two in the fall and two in the Spring along with my internship and, if necessary, one additional course. That will put me on target for a smooth year and spring graduation", she thought to herself. "I'll take a graduate exam course and take the test so that I can hurry up and apply to grad school", Racquel thought.

Racquel had always been so encouraging of what everyone else wanted to do with their careers, that she initially half-heartedly chose her own major. It wasn't supply chain management, it wasn't public health or criminal justice, it wasn't biomedical engineering. She wasn't interested in law school and didn't really envision herself in a cubicle sitting at a computer all day. Racquel liked to research and pull data and stats but that would put her behind a computer and have her wearing reading glasses by the age of 35. Racquel wasn't a math whiz so several majors were off the table for her. She finally narrowed it down to Sociology and Communications.

Racquel decided to major in Communications with a focus on Social Media Management. More and more companies were hiring individuals to handle their social media platforms. They were hiring people to post and respond to posts and they were paying good money to do it. The best part about a Social Media Management position was that it was often a hybrid position where an employee spent half the time in the office and the other half working from home.

The ability to work from home and not be confined to an office or cubicle is what sealed the deal for Racquel. Even though the skills associated with the position were transferrable, she thought that a master's degree in Public Relations would further enhance her educational background. She was finally figuring it out and she was pleased with herself.

We Made Plans

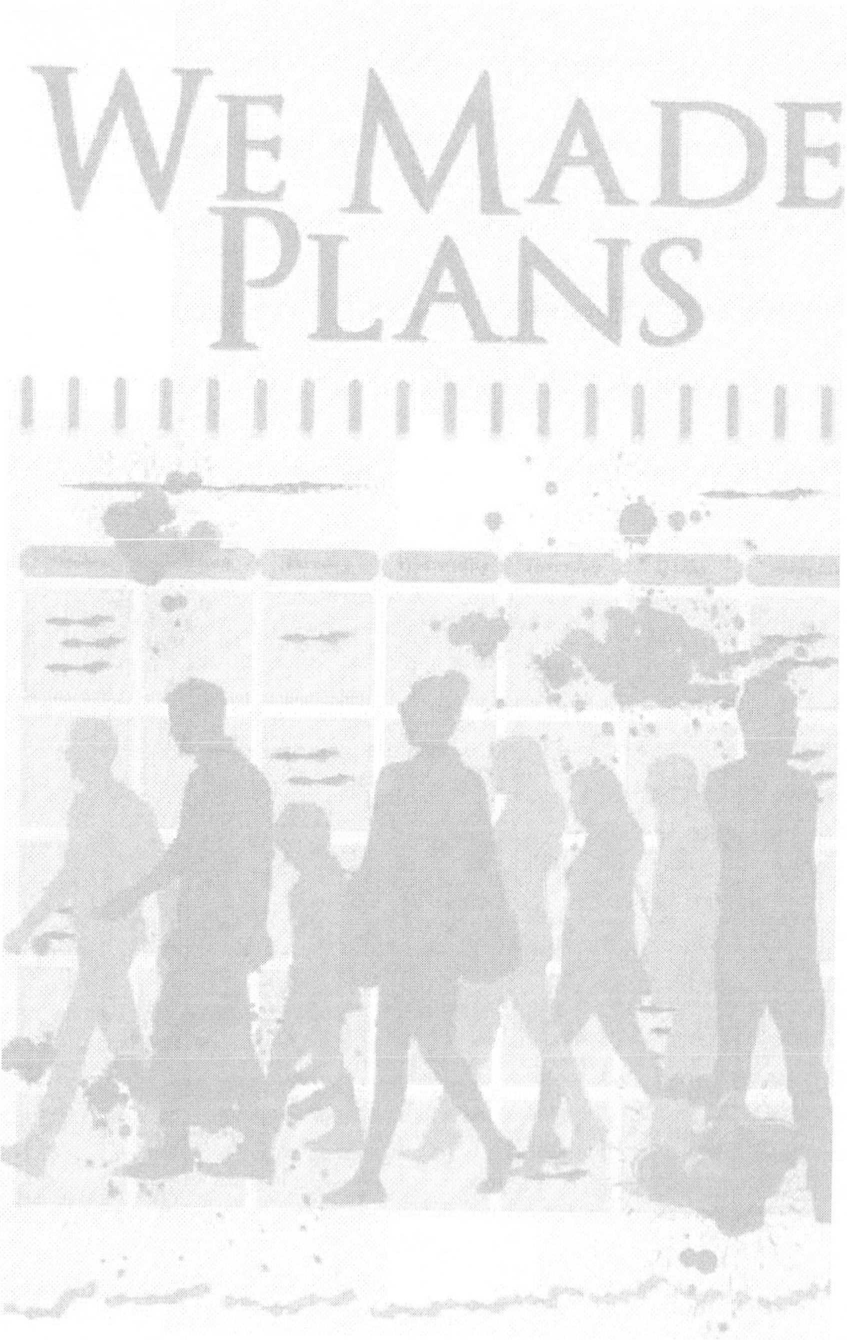

# CHAPTER THIRTEEN

**W**HILE RACQUEL AND HER FRIENDS** were living their best lives their senior year of college, someone had given birth to the devil himself 15 years prior. If Racquel could go back in time, she would go back to the day and moment that kid was about to be conceived and somehow stop it!

Roy Kenneth Holtz was the fifth of six children, born in a small town in Virginia. His father had gun permits and owned several varieties of weapons from pistols and Glocks to assault rifles. In fact, when the Public Safety and Recreational Firearms Use Protection Act, which banned the manufacturing for civilian use of certain semi-automatic assault weapons and large capacity ammunition magazines, lapsed in 2004, Roy's Dad leapt at the opportunity to stock up. He maintained a locked storage shed of firearms and ammunition. He taught all his boys at an early age how to clean, handle, shoot and respect guns. Somewhere along the line, Roy's heart calcified, and he became obsessed with guns and killing.

Maybe it was the combination of mindlessly violent video games and the access to his father's weapons. Maybe it was the constant bullying from the middle school kids that set him on his treacherous path of destruction. Perhaps it was because he was the 5th of 6 children and suffered from intentional or unintentional parental neglect. Perhaps it was his access to the internet and the start of becoming radicalized.

Perhaps it was his growing hatred of all people unlike himself. There seemingly could have been 100 different reasons why Roy Kenneth Holtz decided to do what he did! The intricate details of his life are insignificant prior to the time he made a lasting impact on Racquel's.

*"Be sober, be vigilant; because your adversary the devil, as a roaring lion, walketh about, seeking whom he may devour:" 1 Peter 5:8 KJV*

# CHAPTER FOURTEEN

CHRISTMAS IN NY WAS always a wonderful time and they looked forward to it. Mo was able to go with them again because he had a few days off prior to Christmas. His team would literally fly to Texas on Christmas morning to start practicing for a December 29th Bowl game. The day moved along as usual. They stopped at Kelly's, now off campus apartment, to drop off their bags and then they headed to the City. They stopped for their dirty dogs, topped with chili, cheese, sauerkraut, relish, etc. depending on whose hotdogs you were looking at. They picked up plenty of napkins and Kelly had wet wipes as well. They were better prepared compared to their first visit.

The first stop was Rockefeller Center to see the Christmas tree and watch the ice skaters. It was so crowded in the streets that they almost had to walk single file to get through. They took pictures in front of the tree again and put pics on social media right away. Racquel demanded they all be consistent with the hashtags. Racquel and Brandon did not get snagged by the cartoon giants like they had a couple of years earlier. They were smarter and savvier now. They made their way over to Madison Square Garden to take pics there again with Mo's arms stretched wide. This year he wanted to take a picture with Racquel with their arms stretched wide. Raquel obliged and Brandon snapped the picture.

# We Made Plans

They were having a great time! Zeke suggested they venture out to Brooklyn to this cool restaurant he wanted them to check out. He said it was in a good area and that there would be no worries. "There's a lot of young professionals and it's been gentrified", Zeke said with a laugh. That statement commenced a heated debate between he and Mo. Mo was annoyed that Zeke would think that because a neighborhood that used to be predominantly black but was now taken over by young white people, would be more appealing to them as African Americans. He wondered why they should feel safer around white people than black people. The debate ended with Kelly, the level-headed mediator, suggesting they agree to disagree and move on.

They headed out to Brooklyn taking the C-Train to Jay Street-Metro Tech Station, near Fulton Street. The streets were lined with oversized Christmas ornaments on the light posts and lights strung across the street from post to post. It was crowded but not as bad as the city. They could walk coupled up with no problems.

They dipped into a literal hole in the wall of a restaurant. It had a glass front window with a rectangular sign above it that read SWEET SHUGGS and flashed the word OPEN in neon colors. They entered a brick interior with no ceiling, just exposed lighting and duct work. It was about 80 feet deep excluding the kitchen and maybe 30 feet wide. A pretty, slim, shapely girl with long box braids (1B/30) down to the small of her back greeted them and said, Welcome to Sweet Shuggs! How many?" Clearly, she did not eat the cuisine served at Sweet Shuggs.

She walked like a model on a runway with shoulders back and one leg crossing in front of the other. She cat-walked the six of them back to their large booth to accommodate six to eight people.

Mo always faced the doors; never sitting with his back to a door. Raquel sat next to him on the inside followed by Candice, Brandon, Kelly and Zeke.

An equally handsome male waiter appeared. He looked as if he were a male model at about 6 ft tall, abs and an extremely slim, muscular build. Clearly, he didn't eat the cuisine served at Sweet Shuggs either. He recognized Zeke, shook hands with him and proceeded to take their order. Two orders of Sweet's fried chicken and waffles for Racquel and Mo with a side of candied yams that they would split, but Mo didn't know it at the time he ordered. Kelly and Candice ordered Mr. Jenkins' shrimp n grits.

Racquel preferred her Daddy's shrimp n grits and after a while refused to order anyone else's. She said it was a waste of her money. Brandon ordered Shugg's smothered turkey wings, potato salad and cabbage. Zeke ordered Rohan's Jerk chicken, mac n cheese and collard greens. Zeke also ordered the table the appetizer sampler of fried chicken wings, jerk chicken wings and buffalo chicken wings, each with its own homemade dipping sauce; a thousand island type sauce for the fried, a chutney for the jerk and blue cheese dressing for the buffalo. Brandon ordered two pitchers of Sweet Shugg's house punch. The food itself and the presentation was spectacular!

Everyone laughed and talked for another 2 hours. Racquel thought it was the perfect time to tell everyone that she and Mo were a couple but absolutely no one was surprised. Apparently, Mo told his confidant Brandon and told him not to tell anyone, but Bandon told Candice and told her not to say anything to Racquel or Sydney. Racquel confided in Kelly and she told Zeke so Racquel and Mo's little announcement was a dud. Everyone already knew. So much for Mo and Racquel keeping their relationship a secret.

# We Made Plans

Before they left the restaurant, Mo ordered dessert to go for everyone, so they left with huge, generous slices of sweet potato pie, lemon cake, red velvet cake, carrot cake, cheesecake and chocolate cake. That hole in the wall restaurant was a culinary delight! Racquel knew she needed to get back to Brooklyn sooner rather than later to visit Sweet Shuggs again. Mo complimented Zeke on his restaurant choice and thanked him. To which, they all said. "Yes, great choice!", "Yessss!", and "yeah thanks Zeke!"

Everyone pooled their money and just took an Uber back to Kelly's place. It was almost 3:30 in the morning by the time they arrived, and everyone was exhausted.

Zeke was heading out to Kelly's house for Christmas and Candice was headed out to Brandon's, so they all got about 5 hours of sleep before they picked up the SUV for the drive and hit the road for home. Another NYC trip under their belts. No problems and no cares in the world!

# CHAPTER FIFTEEN

**T**HEY DIDN'T BUY VERY MANY GIFTS IN NY because of their busy itinerary. When they arrived home, they said their hello's and greeted everyone before they headed back out to the local mall. They had to go early because they were expecting snow later in the evening.

They went to the same mall where they often frequented since high school. Again, they peaked into some stores, bought a few items and spent most of their time in the food court. They saw old classmates who "just knew" Racquel and Mo would end up together. Racquel and Mo smiled and pretended it was great to see some people and were genuinely happy to see others.

Racquel didn't let Mo trick her into buying her own gift. He would have to figure it out on his own this year. She was going to buy Mo a gift later in the day or the next day when she was by herself.

Brandon and Candice needed to get away from Brandon's house because his Mom was a little territorial when it came to Brandon and was not as hospitable as one would hope when they bring a significant other home for the parent to meet. So, they met Racquel and Mo at the food court for their usual deli sandwiches, pizza, wings, chicken fingers and Thai food. Kelly and Zeke weren't sure if they were going to make it out of the house because, of course, things were going great over there. Racquel told them what time they expected to leave the mall in case they wanted to head out before then. Racquel also mentioned to Kelly that they were sitting in the corner of the food court near the entrance to JC Penny and to text her if she wasn't over there. Kelly said it was also going to start snowing later so she wasn't sure what they were going to do.

In the meantime, Brandon, Mo, and Racquel were discussing their flight out on December 28th to go to Texas for the Bowl game. They were headed out on the morning of the 28th. Brandon and Racquel planned on enjoying the good Texas BBQ compliments of Racquel's parents' generous yearly monetary Christmas gift. Mo would have time for them for about 3 hours mid-afternoon. Otherwise, the team would be in meetings, practices and had an early curfew the night before the game.

After that, they wouldn't see Mo again until he went back home after the game. It was going to be Racquel and Brandon like when they were in elementary school and before middle school when Kelly entered the scene, before H.S when Mo entered the scene and before College when Brandon lost his mind over Candice. Candice chimed in about wanting to go with them but realistically she wouldn't see Brandon again until he returned to school in mid January.

Brandon and Mo started talking about the upcoming game and how Mo had to be in beast mode because it's a make or break year, and how he had to finish strong. Brandon was Mo's unofficial coach, manager, hype man and his official personal comedian. They often checked in with each other several times a week, via text or a call. Brandon and Mo were like brothers and no matter who would come and go, they would always be there for each other.

Candice surprisingly saw Kelly and Zeke walking into the food court and stood up to wave them over. Racquel turned to look and saw Kelly and Zeke headed over to their table.

They hugged, kissed and greeted each other as if they hadn't seen each other for an entire semester. It was literally just a few hours prior. Mo motioned for them to sit down but Kelly wanted to grab a mocha latte from the coffee bar first so they said they would be right back and wanted to know if anyone wanted anything. Everyone politely declined.

Brandon and Mo continued their conversation while Candice and Racquel scrolled through social media on their phones. They were still tallying up likes from all their annual NYC Christmas pics and checking to see who liked which pics and what comments, if any, were left. Candice laughed at a meme and showed it to Racquel. A minute or so later, Candice turned her phone around to show Racquel a funny dog video. Racquel watched and laughed at the short video and then heard what sounded like firecrackers in the middle of the mall.

Candice jumped and her phone fell out of her hand. Racquel briefly thought to herself, "Who is setting off firecrackers in December?" As she simultaneously looked up from the phone to see what was going on, Mo immediately slammed her head down on the table and tackled her to the floor of the food court. He scrambled on the floor with one arm around her dragging her under him and the other helping him to bear claw his way to a column not too far away from where they were sitting.

71

# We Made Plans

Racquel heard more firecrackers and was a little dazed from the blow to the head. What turned out to be gunshots became louder and louder. People were screaming. Children immediately started crying and yelling in sheer terror. Everyone started to run and stampede. There was total chaos and panic in the food court. She could hear bullets penetrating walls and drywall and debris hitting the ground. She heard large thumps from people crashing to the ground after being shot and unable to brace their fall. Racquel's heart was pounding as she started to realize that someone was in the food court shooting at people ... two days before Christmas.

Mo was holding her so tight; she could barely breathe. She felt his heart pounding as well. His chest was heaving. He said to Racquel, "when the shots stop, we're running for that exit right there to your right. Racquel looked over at the exit and the bright red sign above it. It was only about 20 feet away, but it seemed like a mile considering the circumstances.

Racquel said ok and Mo said "shhhhhhh!" shots rang out and she could hear more tables and chairs scraping across the ground as people tried to take cover. It sounded like a chaotic scene but Racquel couldn't see anything. Then the shots stopped. Maybe it was a jam or time for a reload. Mo picked Raquel up like a football and took off toward the exit. Raquel's feet did not touch the floor at all. She was nearly horizontal to the ground and Mo was sprinting. She was like a rag doll in his arms. More shots rang out. Raquel felt her shoulder and leg bang against the wall by the exit as Mo continued to sprint up the hallway.

The gunman was relentless firing at random at the young, old and everyone in between. Racking up a high body count seemed to be his only objective. He had two semi-automatic guns, maybe an AK 47 style, a high powered 40 caliber Glock with an extended clip, and a cache of ammunition to take hundreds of shots, along with two hunting knives.

Mo busted through an exit door that led to the outside. He adjusted his grip on Raquel and ran behind some cars. His chest was heaving, and he was scared senseless. Racquel was out of breath; not from any running she had to do but Mo's grip around her rib cage was crushing. Racquel tried to gain her composure. She looked around and yelled, "where's everybody?" Mo looked at her confused and dazed. "Where's Brandon, Candice, Kelly and Zeke?" she yelled.

Mo looked at Racquel dumbfounded and yelled, "oh shit!" He peeked out from around the car where he crouched and saw some more people running out of the same exit door. He scanned the parking lot looking for any signs of their friends. They heard sirens in the distance, but they could still hear rapidly firing gunshots. Racquel was hysterical at the thought of an active shooter in the mall two days before Christmas. She knew for a fact that some people died or were dying, and she didn't know where the rest of her friends were.

Mo grabbed Racquel and hugged her tight, almost smothering her in the hood of his sweatshirt. She was still trying to catch her breath when Mo yelled, "WHAT THE FUCK!" with added emphasis on "fuck" "Your leg is bleeding!" At the very moment he said it, the pain in Racquel's leg intensified. Up until that point, Racquel had not felt a thing. She had been shot in her calf and hadn't realized it. When she looked at the destruction to her leg, she nearly passed out. She threw her head back and laid out on the cold ground and the first snowflake fell directly onto her eyelash.

Mo remembered that the legs have vital arteries but didn't know if a vital artery was hit. Raquel felt unimaginable pain and just laid on the ground, breathing heavy and crying. She closed her eyes. Mo yelled, "Raquel, Do NOT close your eyes, you're going to be ok. It's not a major artery. I know it hurts but you're going to be ok." Raquel felt some comfort in his words. Mo was lying but Racquel didn't know it!

Mo quickly realized he had to stop the bleeding, so he took off his hoodie and with trembling hands pressed it against her leg. Mo remembered that he took a course where an instructor from "Bleeding control.org" came in to discuss how to handle a situation where someone is suffering from uncontrollable bleeding and how regular non-medical people could help prevent them from bleeding out by minimizing or stopping the bleeding until paramedics arrived.

Mo was tired that day in class, but he paid attention because it was especially interesting. He didn't want to be a doctor or anything because the sight of excessive blood was a little disturbing to him, but he thought it was good knowledge to have in case he or one of his boys (male friends) ever got shot. The last thing he thought was that he would have to use it on his girlfriend during a mass shooting.

Mo didn't quite remember the details of how to make a tourniquet in terms of how far above the wound he should place and tighten the device and he didn't have a pen or anything to write down the time he set the tourniquet. More importantly, he wasn't even wearing a belt. There was no way he could tie the sweatshirt tight enough, so he just pressed it into her leg. She was NOT going to bleed out.

# La Onque Chavette

The temperature outside was about 30 degrees. Mo was only wearing a short-sleeved t-shirt under his hoodie. The snow, earlier than anticipated, began to fall more steadily. He didn't feel the cold or the snow.

Racquel couldn't believe that she was shot. She started to think about how the gunman tried to take them out but only caught her calf. He deliberately and callously shot at them. If Mo was a half-step slower, he could have been shot. Racquel finally asked him if he was ok and he said he wasn't hit. He squatted behind the car and looked around.

The police arrived and immediately entered the building wearing protective gear and with guns drawn. More people began to run out of the mall with both hands in the air and were ushered over to a holding area about 400 yards away toward one of the parking garages. Someone yelled "Mo", crying and yelling "Mo". It was Candice coming from the other direction. Mo asked her "you ok?" "where's Brandon?" She said she didn't know. Mo's stomach started to ache. Candice said she didn't see where he ran but she ran through the Chinese food store and out their back door.

She was crying hysterically. Mo stopped her and told her that Racquel was hit and she screamed and said, "Oh my God!" Candice dropped her phone during all the chaos so she couldn't call 911 or home or anywhere. Several additional cop cars, and ambulances started to pull up. Mo waved the paramedics over to Racquel, pointed out her leg and handed Racquel over to the paramedics.

Racquel told him to stay with Candice and find everybody else. He asked which hospital they were taking Racquel to, told her he would be there soon and that he would call her parents. A paramedic quickly surveyed Mo and Candice for injury, handed Mo a blanket and moved on to other victims. A couple of minutes later the very intimidating SWAT trucks pulled up to the mall.

They could not go back into the mall because it was an active crime scene, so they just had to wait indefinitely. Candice was still crying hysterically, and Mo tried to console her. He wiped Racquel's blood off his hands and onto the blanket. He took Candice by the hand and walked over to someone with a phone and asked if he could use it. They let him call his mom and dad to tell them that he was ok. His parents were still unaware that the shooting occurred.

His Dad immediately turned on the news to try to get more information. His mom asked if Racquel was ok, so he told them that Racquel had been shot in the leg, what hospital she was headed to and asked them to contact the Wilsons. Mo also said, "Mom, I don't know where Brandon, Kelly, and Zeke are. Candice is with me and unharmed. Please pray that they're ok." Mo's mom said that she would. They hung up the phone and Mo's mom immediately called Racquel's parents and then began to call and text other family and friends. Mo had Candice calm down and call her family to let them know she was ok.

Candice wanted to call Brandon's cell phone, but Mo stopped her and said that if Brandon was hiding and forgot to silence his phone, she would draw attention to him. Candice said, "But I don't hear anymore gunshots!" Mo told her it didn't matter and to be patient and that Brandon was going to be ok. Ten or Fifteen minutes after the first shots, that sounded like firecrackers, rang out, Candice said, "Oh my God, what about Kelly and Zeke!! Where are they?"

The delay was understandable. Kelly was Racquel and Mo's friend from school and Zeke was her boyfriend. The connection was not as deep for Candice, although she liked them both. Mo said, "I don't know but everyone is going to be ok." He hugged her and comforted her. Mo was cold. Candice said, "Mo we have to get into the warmth before you freeze to death. We're not going to survive a mass shooting for you to freeze to death. Racquel wouldn't have it!"

Mo stated, "I'm ok." Then he suddenly reached into his pocket and grabbed his car keys. "Let's go to my car for now." Mo opened his trunk, grabbed a bottle of water and washed Racquel's blood off his hands. He looked down at his bloodied shirt and pants. Then he felt the magnitude of what was happening deep in his stomach. A chilling, overwhelming feeling made him shiver. He abruptly turned away from the open trunk and vomited off the side of the car.

The gunman, Roy Kenneth Holtz, committed suicide after wreaking havoc on the mall two days before Christmas. The news reported nine people were killed and 26 others injured. They deliberately excluded the 15-year-old gunman from their total count. Racquel was one of the injured but she was alive.

We Made Plans

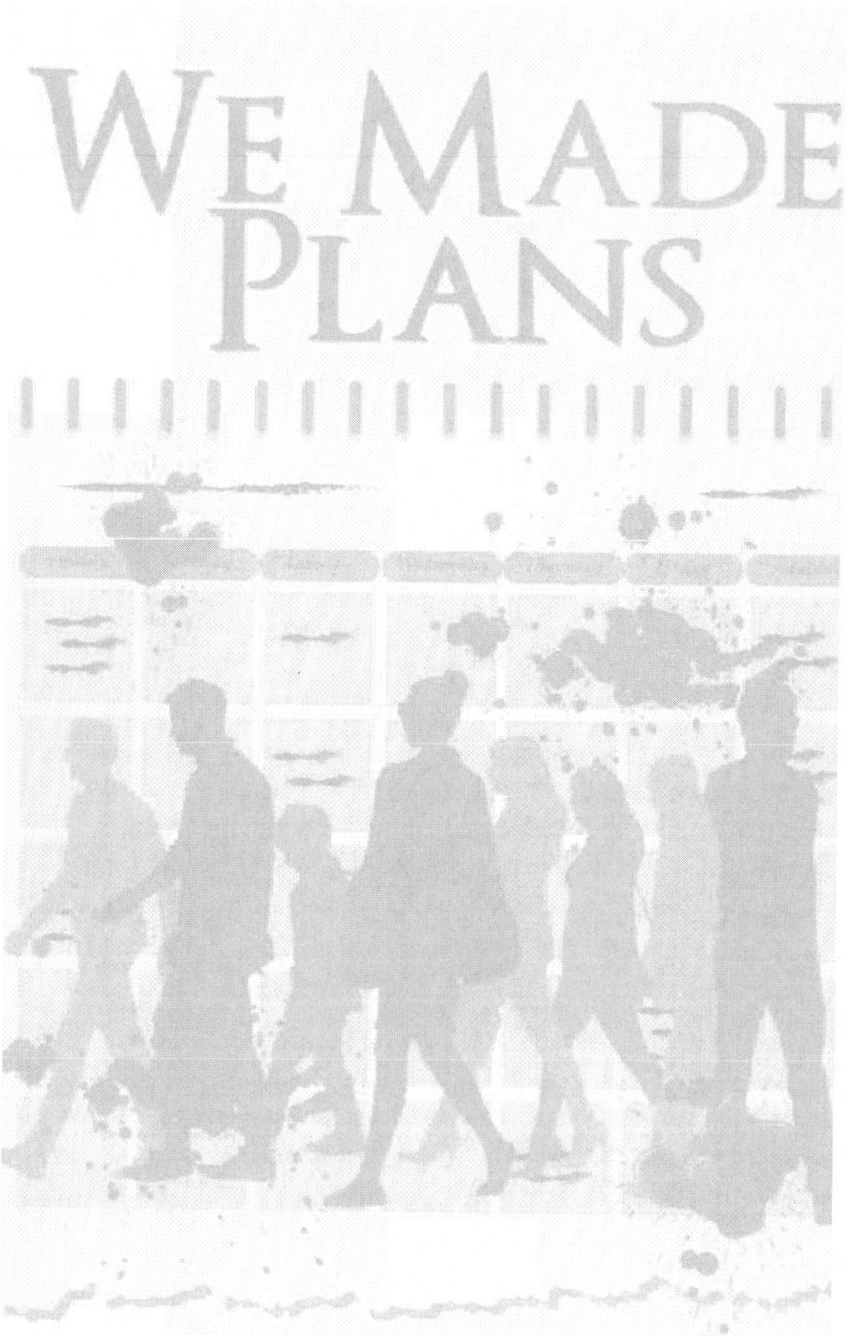

## CHAPTER SIXTEEN

**T**HANKFULLY, THE CANDLE STORE WAS just around the corner from the food court and Kelly wanted to pick up a few of the popular 3-wick, jar candles as gifts before getting her mocha latte from the coffee cafe. Customers weren't allowed to have beverages in the candle store. So, Kelly decided to wait to get the lattes until after they finished up at the other store. Then they would sit down with her friends and enjoy their lattes and maybe a Cinnabon.

That decision took Kelly and Zeke out of the direct line of sight and fire of the gunman. As soon as the shots were fired, the manager pushed an alarm button that dropped the gate and locked everyone in. Everyone was ushered out the back exit through a long corridor that led to a loading dock. They took cover behind the back of the mall. Zeke and Kelly were untouched, fully covered, protected and unharmed.

*My sheep hear my voice, and I know them, and they follow me*
*And I give unto them eternal life; and they shall never perish, neither shall any man pluck them out of my hand"*
*John 10:27-28 KJV*

79

# We Made Plans

Raquel was taken to University State Medical Center, a level 1 trauma center. They immediately triaged and prepped Racquel for surgery. She underwent surgery before her family arrived at the hospital. The snow had picked up and there was close to a ½ inch on the ground, so her family was forced to drive a little slower on the slick and slushy roads.

It drove her Dad insane that he was unable to get there any faster than he did. His stomach ached, his heart was racing, and he was trying to remain calm. He didn't want to give himself a heart attack, but he was concerned about his baby girl. He felt like he was going to cry but he swallowed hard and did not shed a tear.

By the time Racquel was out of surgery and recovering, her family, Mo and Candice had been there for a while. They were there praying and waiting for her to wake up post-surgery. Racquel's leg felt weird, not painful because she was heavily drugged, but weird. She woke up briefly and long enough to see her parents but went right back to sleep. She didn't dream anything; she was just in a deep sleep.

Racquel woke up on the morning of Christmas Eve and when she realized what happened, she cried. She cried for the people she knew died the day before; for the people who lost their loved ones so close to Christmas.

She thought about how the gifts purchased for loved ones would remain unopened while they instead planned funerals. Racquel cried even harder when she thought about how she and Mo's life had been spared. Those were tears of joy and praise to God for the gift of life and health. Then she began to think about the plans she made for that day, Christmas Day and the day after that.  Racquel Amani Wilson and her family, and her friends, and so many other people made plans for that day.

# CHAPTER SEVENTEEN

THE DAY RACQUEL PERSONALLY FACED A LIFE or death situation, all she could think about was that she had made plans for that day! She was supposed to head back to the mall without Mo to get his Christmas gift. It would have been the first gift she bought for him and she wanted it to be thoughtful and something that would make him smile. Mo had full, perfectly shaped lips and a handsome smile that lit up the room. Despite his intimidating looks in general, his genuine smile puts everyone at ease.

The next day on Christmas Eve, Raquel would have been baking a few batches of cookies and preparing her Mom's potato salad for Christmas dinner. Her mom demanded she learn and practice making the potato salad because she believed a woman should have several recipes she cooked well. Potato salad was one of Racquel's specialties.

It was also guaranteed that Raquel or one of her siblings would inevitably have to make one or more runs to the local grocery store and wrap a few last-minute stocking stuffers. Her evening would have been topped off with a yearly Bible reading from the book of Luke, family prayer, the opening of the stocking stuffers and the opening of one parent-approved, pre-selected gift. Raquel would have been surrounded by family, the people who loved her and those she loved. She made plans for that day to continue the traditions her family had maintained throughout the years and to enjoy every moment of it.

A few days after that, Raquel and Brandon were supposed to be flying to Mo's Bowl game in Texas. It would have been her first time in Texas, and they were going to eat lots of the infamous Texas BBQ. Raquel planned on sampling their ribs, pulled pork, brisket, baked beans, and string beans with sweeeeet cornbread. She was even going to try Texas mac n cheese.

She was going to eat until she had to unbutton her jeans to relieve her bloated belly. She and Brandon were supposed to be there to cheer their best friend and his teammates on in his first collegiate bowl game. They made plans for that day and the gunman, Roy Kenneth Holtz, took that away from them. "Bastard! I know he is rotting in hell", Racquel angrily thought to herself.

# CHAPTER EIGHTEEN

THERE ARE SO MANY CLICHÉS ABOUT the brevity of life. They say life is short. They say you only live once. They say, and Racquel had heard, a lot of things about life, life span, quality of life, and living your best life. Suddenly, the clichés had new meaning. "But what does any of it really mean?" Racquel thought to herself. Certainly, she understood that your life could end in an unexpected instant and in an inconceivable way.

So, what good are any of those little clichés about life when you're faced with a life and death situation. In that moment of survive or die, kill or be killed, and split decision situations staring you in the face, what do you do or think about? Maybe those little clichés are to encourage you to appreciate the beauty of life while you're living.

When Racquel thought back to the previous day's events and how everything unfolded, she realized that if not for Mo's quick actions, she may have died that day. She may have been number ten.

Some people are professionally trained to know exactly what to do. They've rehearsed it, practiced it, conducted drills for it. They've literally given their own blood sweat and tears to know exactly what to do in a life or death situation. Their goal is to neutralize or terminate the threat and survive. At the end of the day, the ultimate aim is to walk away and head back to the people and things they love. Police departments and law enforcement conduct drills. Hospitals, schools and workplaces conduct trainings and drills.

Others are constantly on the lookout for signs of trouble. Their daily routine is consumed with "where's the nearest exit. How many exits are there? If that exit is blocked, what's my next option. Who looks suspicious? Who is trying not to look too suspicious but could be a potential perpetrator? What can I use for cover? Their eyes shift up to the exit signs, scan the room and return quickly to what's in front of them. They look back and over their shoulder briefly to check who entered behind them.

When they take a seat, they take note of who is near. These people watch the cars pulling up to the restaurant. They watch the people who run out of the movie theater for more popcorn or a bathroom break, and they cautiously await their return. They wait and watch, and they have a plan of what to do should anyone around them attempt to wreak havoc. These people make observations in the first few seconds of entering a location. They'll do it quietly, in their mind, without anyone having a clue as to what they're thinking.

The well trained and the increasingly paranoid may survive or they may die trying to selflessly help everyone else. But one thing for sure is that they've rehearsed it in their minds and know exactly what they're going to do in several different scenarios. They work on mental muscle memory the same as athletes who train their bodies daily for the big event.

There are yet others, who don't give it any thought. They live their lives happy as a chipmunk, constantly checking the last picture posted on social media to see how many likes they've received in the past 10 minutes and then checking to see if their favorite person or someone who just followed them has liked the picture yet. These people don't check for exits and bright exit signs. They don't scan the rooms they enter. They rarely look up from their phones to see where they're going, much less to make eye contact to say hi to the person approaching them from the opposite direction.

These people have never been trained in the armed forces and totally skip any workplace violence and active shooter response training, where survival options and techniques to identify potential threats and how to respond, are offered. They live by the motto of "Do You" and are unbelievably oblivious to their surroundings, unless they are approaching their favorite coffee café. They are also unbothered by the thought of life and death situations because, well, that could never really happen to them.

We Made Plans

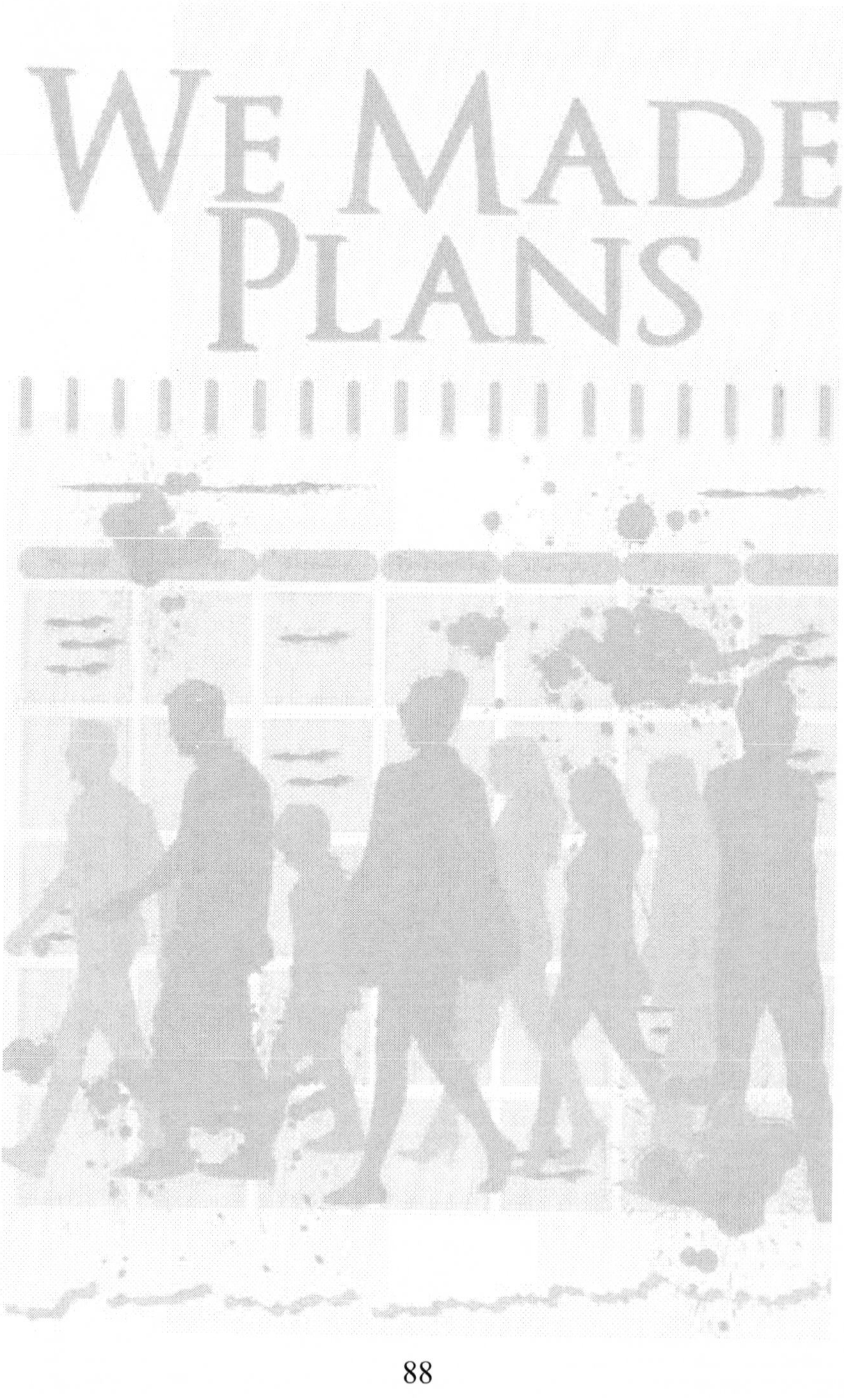

# CHAPTER NINETEEN

**B**RANDON ALWAYS MADE QUESTIONABLE choices and the day of the shooting was no different. He and several others ran towards the JC Penny behind the gunman's back, but the relentless gunman turned around and had several targets to choose from. He picked them off quickly aiming for their heads and shot and killed a couple right there at the entrance to the store. Blood and brains splattered on the clothing, walls, and clothing racks and their hopes and dreams for their future were instantly cut down forever. Brandon survived the active shooter, but he too was one of the 26 injured.

Brandon was shot in the upper back right shoulder. He was able to continue to run further into the store and out of the gunmen's view before he collapsed, partially hidden under a clothing rack and decided to pretend to play dead. Brandon lost a lot of blood waiting for the paramedics to get to him. He truly thought he was going to die.

The other 24 injured people were either shot or trampled and sustained, in addition to critical gunshot wounds, fractures, breaks, concussions and a host of other injuries. The next day all the news channels had the names, ages and hometowns along with flattering, smiling pictures of the decedents. Pictures that they had willfully taken while enjoying their lives, totally unaware that this picture would be used to capture their essence, their love for life, and their vitality in a news report ... about their senseless death. People don't take pictures with the thought of, if I die, use this one. Or do they?

They displayed their pictures across three by three like the Brady Bunch intro as they announced their names.

1.  Carl Buckingham, (white male) age 62, Father of 4 and grandfather of six

2.  Olivia Buckingham, (white female) age 59, Wife to Carl for 35 years

3.  Jipsani Momar, (Asian-Indian female) age 23, Graduate student

4.  Fred Smith, (black male) age 34, Corporate executive and Father of 2 including a 1-year old baby boy

5.  William (Mr. Billy) Connors, (black male) age 71, Mall security guard, father of 2 and grandfather of 4. He was apparently the first one shot and didn't stand a chance at getting away because the gunman walked up to him from behind, in a back hallway near the food court, put the Glock behind his head and fired. No one recalls hearing that gunshot because the mall was so crowded and loud at the time. Mr. Billy knew and spoke to all the mall regulars. He was a good guy.

6.  Juanita Sinclair, (black female) age 44, Mother of 4, PTA President

7.   Cassidy Winston, (white female) age 12, Middle schooler and gymnastics star

8.   Adami Ngozi, (black male) age 26, Law school student

9.   Alexa Vasquez (Puerto Rican female), age 17, HS Volleyball star, college bound senior


All Nine of those people and their families, made plans for that day. Now their families were planning funerals. By the time the new year would roll in, the stories would be dropped, and the next news stories would be told. The families alone would be left to deal with the aftermath and the deep, stomach aching, heart wrenching, unimaginable pain and sorrow of dealing with the tragic, senseless, sudden loss of their loved ones. Only those who have experienced this loss, one way or another, would understand their pain. Everyone else would just empathize with them and continue living their lives. After all, life must go on. But for those who know the pain, they know.

# We Made Plans

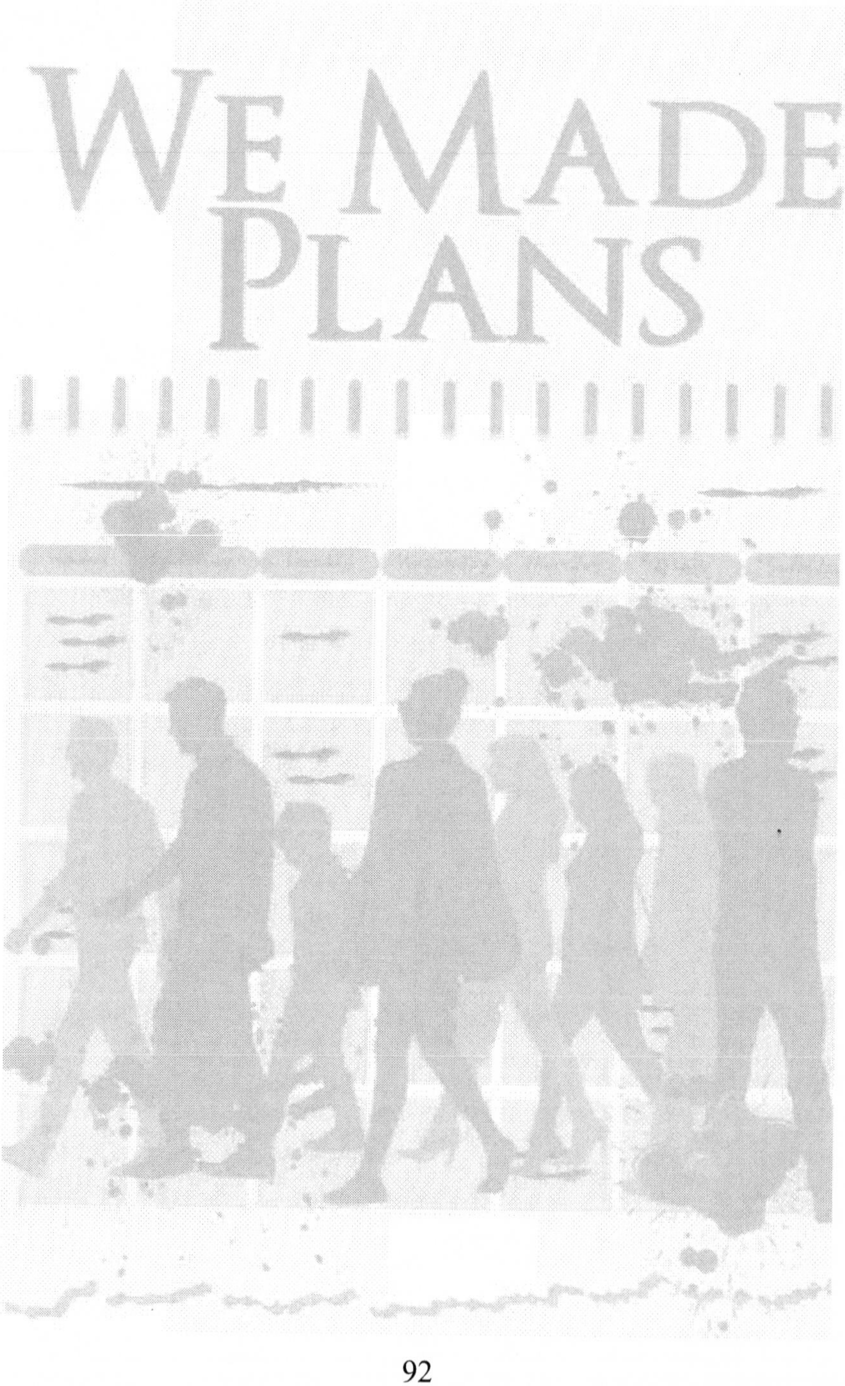

# CHAPTER TWENTY

**M**O DIDN'T WANT TO LEAVE RAQUEL'S SIDE but both his parents and Racquel's parents convinced him to get ready to leave for Christmas Day. They encouraged him to refocus his attention long enough to ball out for the game and reminded him that his future depended on it.

When Racquel awoke and was more coherent, Mo talked to her about leaving and promised that he would stay and be with her if she wanted him to. Racquel smiled at Mo and said, "Mo you were my protector that day and I love you for that. I want the best for you and don't want you to miss out on this opportunity. You have to go". Mo held Racquel's hand and started smiling almost laughing.

Once again Racquel had to ask. In a weakened voice, she said, "why are you laughing at me?" Mo said, "Nothing, I just... I just love you too". Racquel said to him, you would have helped anyone near you that day. Mo raised his eyebrows, then grimaced and said, "Mmmm I don't know about that Roc. I didn't grab for Candice. I only thought about keeping you safe." Then he paused and said, "I mean thank God Candice was ok, but I seriously didn't think twice about her. I was just trying to get us out of there."

"I'm not a hero", he said as he lowered his almost hazel eyes. Racquel exclaimed, "God and you were my protector!" I'm going to walk away from this and there are people that can't. I'm thankful for that. All of us are going to be ok." Mo leaned over and gave her a long kiss. He told her that he was going to play for them so that, as much as was in his power to, he would make a better life for them.

Racquel still foggy headed from the anesthesia and pain medicine, thought about the earning potential professional football players had and she thought about asking Mo to adopt her, then she thought about asking him to marry her. Then she thought better. It must be the pain medication because she would never do that. She would wait patiently for him to ask her. Besides, her Dad wouldn't tolerate that anyway. Racquel dosed off to sleep and awoke briefly to the sound of her Dad's voice praying for Mo.

She looked over towards the door where she saw her mom, dad and Mo standing in a circle, holding hands with their heads bowed. She heard her Dad say, "…as he travels to and from his destination… please God continue to protect him, watch over him, keep him healthy and we pray Lord that your will be done in his life, in the precious name of Jesus. Amen, Amen, Amen." Racquel wanted to say something but couldn't muster up the strength. She went back to that deep, black sleep where she didn't dream about anything at all.

Kelly's mom sent Mo a text with a biblical verse that read:

*"The Lord Bless thee, and keep thee: The Lord make his face shine upon thee, and be gracious unto thee: The Lord lift up his countenance upon thee, and give thee peace" Numbers 6:24-26 KJV*

# La Onque Chavette

Mo replied with praying hands and a "thank you so much Mrs. Cook."

Mo squeezed Racquel and kissed her bye as she lay in the hospital bed recovering and she didn't even know it. She was sound asleep.

Christmas Day Mo departed for the airport at 5 am for an 8:30 am flight to Texas. He and 5 other teammates from the area were on the flight. They were happy to see him and had hundreds of questions for him. The flight attendants heard that an active shooter survivor was on the flight, so they announced it and the passengers cheered for him. A reporter was on the flight as well and wanted to interview Mo.

At first, he declined but his teammates talked him into it. Mo and his teammates were offered to be moved to first class and they accepted. Mo appreciated the good will of people when someone was involved in a horrific event. People knew how to step up and look beyond their differences to help someone in need. Mo didn't NEED a first-class seat, but he was, none the less, happy to have it.

Racquel's family arrived at the hospital at the start of visiting hours. Her mom made breakfast and brought a small plate with bacon eggs and a waffle and a plastic container of her Dad's shrimp n grits. Racquel finally realized how hungry she was and devoured her breakfast. The doctor came in to check on Racquel and wished everyone a Merry Christmas. Everyone returned the Christmas love greetings. She said that Racquel should be able to be discharged later in the day if they promised to keep her off her feet for a couple of days.

They would have a nurse come in to show them the procedure to change her bandages and clean the wound.  They also had to arrange a mandatory follow up visit with the doctor in a week and future follow ups with their primary care physician.  Racquel's family was elated that she would not spend all of Christmas day in the hospital. After a quick lesson, her mom and Dad went back home to get things ready for her return.

Later that day, Racquel arrived home to a ton of family, lots of love, and Kelly and Zeke.  Brandon was still in the hospital and Candice's parents came to pick her up that same day of the mall shooting.  Mo had a short break before they went out to explore the town, so he called.  Racquel's mom put him on speaker phone.  They all yelled, "MERRY CHRISTMAS MO!!"

Racquel was happy to be home but was tired of sitting in the wheelchair and just wanted to get to her bed.  The Christmas music, the family dinner, the games and Christmas movies were more exciting this year.  She looked around at her siblings and cousins playing Uno at the kitchen table, her aunts and uncles chatting it up, eating and drinking and she took it all in.  It was life and it was good.

She thought about how the day would have been so extremely different if she were killed a few days earlier.  She choked back tears.  Her Mom saw her, gave her a big hug and rubbed her head as she pressed it against her chest.  Raquel's mom said, "You need some rest baby."  Then she yelled, "Racquel needs her rest so she's going to bed!  Everyone say goodnight to Roc!"

Racquel took her pain medication, and a host of other meds and injections to ensure no blood clots would form.  Then she fell off into a deep sleep.  Her Dad and Mom checked in on her throughout the night, the same as they did when she was a little girl growing up. They loved her and were thankful to God for keeping her safe and alive.

When they closed the door to walk back to their bedroom, Racquel's mom broke down crying and praising God. Her dad just held her and took her to the room so that she wouldn't wake Racquel. He hugged her real tight, rocked her and said, "yes, I know, Praise Him…Praise Him!" Her Dad allowed himself to cry too.

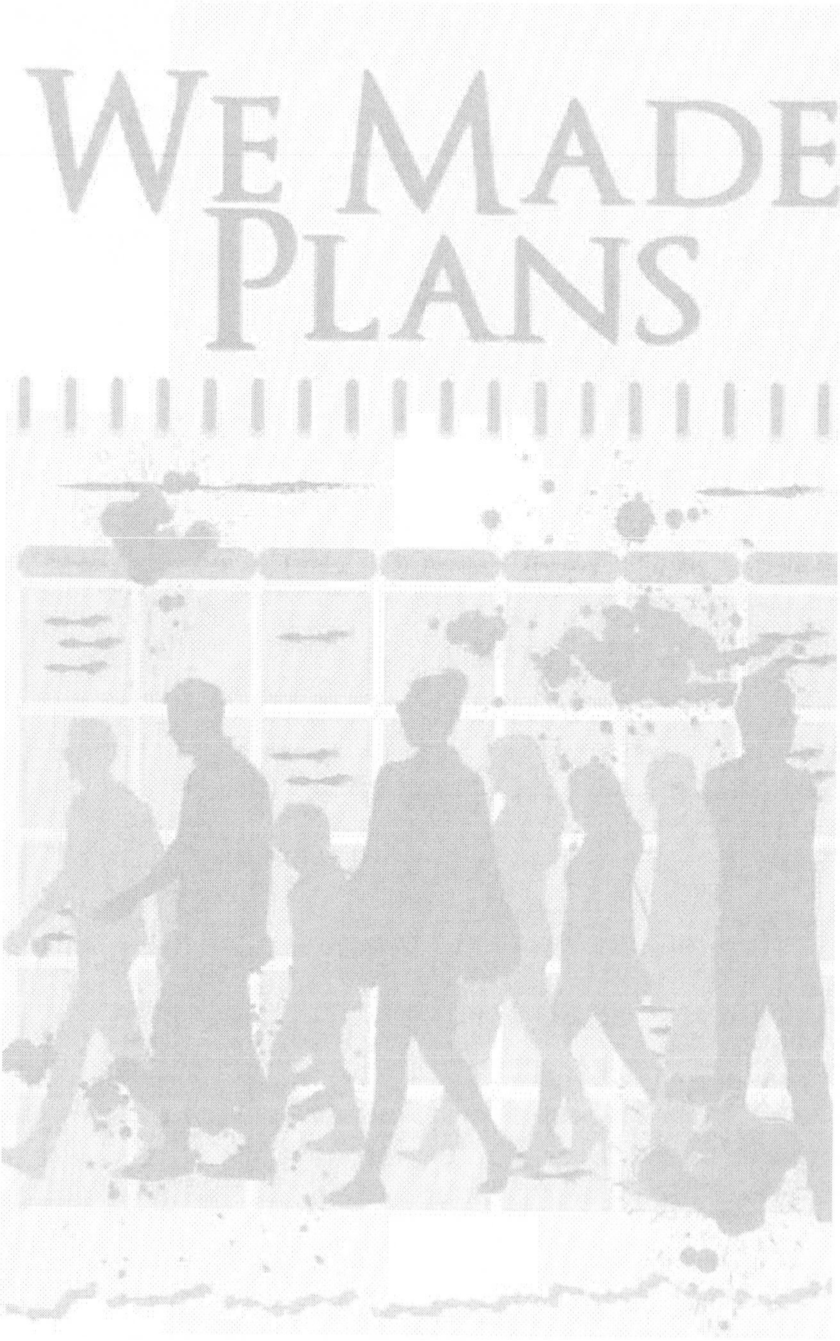
WE MADE PLANS

# CHAPTER TWENTY-ONE

**I**T WAS EARLY JANUARY AND RACQUEL WAS OUT of the wheelchair, had tossed the crutches in a closet but was still walking with a slight limp. The surgeons assured her the limp would go away in due time. Racquel had no worries. She would not be defeated. In a week or so, it would be time to return to school for the last semester. Racquel knew she had to finish strong and get through it for graduation. She refused to let that coward gunman haunt her and ruin her living her best life.

Racquel had not advanced to the admirable stage of forgiveness of the gunman's actions yet, as she had seen so many times on the news. Stoic parents and loved ones standing in front of the cameras saying that they forgive the person who took their loved one from them or even saying that they were praying for the family of that person. Racquel wondered how they could get to a place of forgiveness so quickly. They were literally being interviewed within two days of an event and they were proclaiming forgiveness. Racquel didn't comprehend that and she wasn't there yet. Racquel was happy to believe that he was being tormented in Hell because that's where evil people go when they die. They go to Hell. She believed in Heaven AND Hell.

Brandon and Candice were going through a hell of a time.

# We Made Plans

Candice was not able to get back to see Brandon after that first morning in the hospital. Her parents drove in to pick her up that night but they left immediately on the first morning flight available. Candice's parents couldn't understand why Brandon didn't try to protect her but, rather, ran in the opposite direction. Candice defended him but deep down inside wondered herself. That put a strain on their relationship for a little while.

Brandon was able to redirect her to focus on the fact that they both survived and that if she had gone the same way he did, she could have been shot and injured or shot and killed. He reminded her of the old couple that was shot dead right at the entrance and said that could have been them, but it wasn't. By Valentine's Day, they were back to their regular relationship habits.

Brandon's shoulder ached on and off and he was forced to see a physical therapist three times a week to help get the full rotation back in his arm and shoulder area. Brandon also began to experience disturbing nightmares as a result of the mass shooting. The sounds of people screaming, and the sight of blood everywhere was etched in his mind.

The smell would sometimes creep back into his nasal passages. A peculiar smell of blood and gunpowder or something metallic but he would be the only one to smell it at any given moment. That and the residual pain of the gunshot often kept him up at night. He chose to seek counseling to help him work through the trauma of the experience.

Although Brandon tried to reassure Candice that it was better that she ran in a different direction, he and his therapist spoke at great length about his decision. Brandon confessed that he didn't know what to do or where to run. He acknowledged that things unraveled quickly. "I saw Mo and Racquel hit the ground and scramble and still I wasn't sure what was going on. By the time I realized it, Candice had already taken off running." Brandon looked down and grunted.

After a pause he said, "Actually, Candice left me!... but I would never point that out to her or her parents. I mean there were so many shots being fired… It was total chaos. The way I was sitting on the bench, it was easier for me to get out and run in the direction I did. Otherwise I would've had to run around the tables we were sitting at."

Brandon paused again in deep thought. Then he said, "I wasn't exactly sure where the gunman was when I took off, but I had some sense of where the sounds were coming from, so I just tried to distance myself from the sound of the shots. I was pretty much by myself at that point so I just ran as far away as I could, you know. I was just trying to survive!"

The therapist asked Brandon was he upset with Candice for running and leaving him. Brandon quickly replied, "No, no way, as long as she turned out to be ok and unharmed, I'm not mad about it. I'm glad she went the way she did."

The therapist went on to ask Brandon about what may trigger the smell from the scene. She inquired about what exactly he was doing and where he was located when he experienced the smell sensation. She encouraged Brandon to take note of it and they would discuss further during the next session. She also suggested that Candice accompany him to a couple of sessions, if he felt comfortable with the idea. By April, Candice was going with him to counseling. They were both still traumatized.

We Made Plans

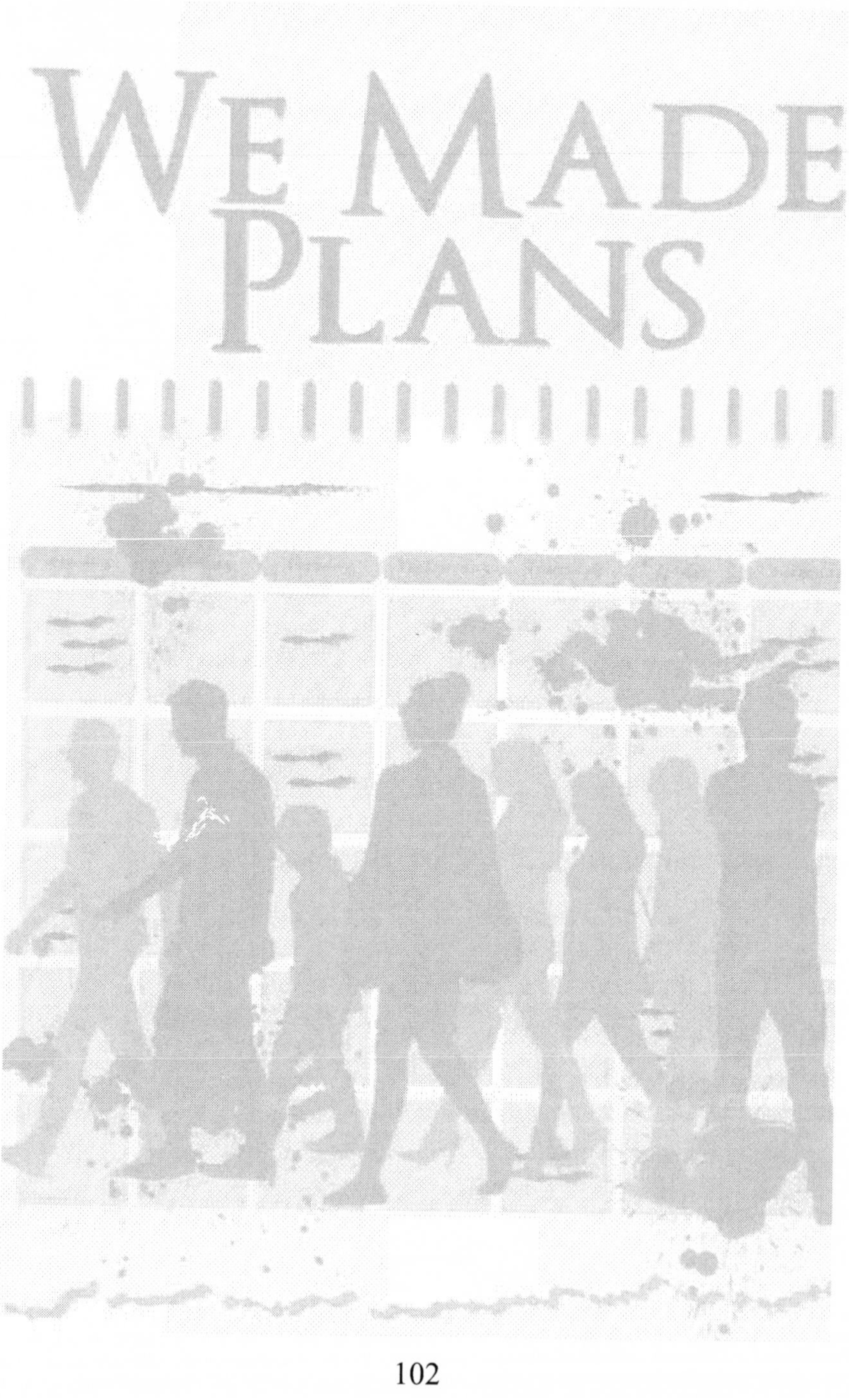

# CHAPTER TWENTY-TWO

**R**ACQUEL WAS DETERMINED TO NOT BE defeated or caught out there in a situation like that again. She got "got", as her parents would say, and she didn't like it. Being the research buff that she was, she started to read reports, studies and accounts of how survivors survived mass shootings. She read and took notes. She constantly shared links with family and friends. She wanted everyone to be aware and to be safe. She could not prevent this from happening again, because active shooter events were on a disturbing rise in the country, but she wanted her friends and family to be aware of how to protect themselves.

Racquel often sat in her dad's favorite leather chair with her legs and feet propped up on the ottoman and read with intensity. Her mouth dropped open as she read the horror stories for which the details were not provided on the news channels. Her eyes filled with tears and often overflowed as she read about the potential lives these people were going to live until their lives were cut short by an active shooter.

Racquel read about the number of shootings that the FBI designated as mass shootings. Certain shootings were excluded and didn't receive the news coverage but certainly were incidents where a perpetrator was "actively involved in killing as many people as possible in a populated area"*. Yet, they didn't make the FBI list.

Two gunmen walked into a closed community art event and shot a total of 10 people with three dying. That one was gang related and didn't make the FBI's list. It seemed like an active shooter/mass shooting event to Racquel but who was she to question the classifications for something as serious as the nation's mass shootings.

Clearly there were historical mass shootings and killings in the country, but those racial incidents weren't included either. The incident some studies reported as one of the first documented mass shootings was at the University of Texas-Austin in 1966 where an ex-military man barricaded himself inside a clock tower, climbed to the top of the tower and took random aim at passersby. He killed 16 people and injured 31 on the University of Texas Austin Campus that day, before the police were able to get to him.

The Columbine school shooting was certainly a popular shooting that created many copycat events referred to as the "Columbine Effect". The Virginia Tech college shooting was also a popular shooting in terms of media coverage. People were lulled into being concerned about mass shootings in reference to institutions of learning and higher education. The reports showed that in the early part of this century close to a quarter of the active shooter events occurred in the school systems. To Racquel's surprise, close to half of the active shooter events occurred in business related locations, not schools. Why didn't she know this! Racquel was a college student and an avid commercial business (mall) supporter.

Why had she been so oblivious to what was happening around her. Movie theaters, churches, malls, dance clubs, yoga studios, café's, restaurants, and open-air concert events became easy targets, with minimal resistance from victims, and an incredible opportunity for huge body counts; sometimes increasing in number by each event. Racquel heard something in the news about some of the events and remembered concerned calls from her parents, but nothing major. She just went about her regular life. She moved freely, without a care in the world, enjoying Mo, her good friends and life.

Racquel discovered that many gunmen in the FBI designated mass shootings obtained their guns legally and were legally registered or licensed to own a gun. The father of the active shooter in the mass shooting Racquel was involved in, was a licensed gun owner. Roy Kenneth Holtz was just a kid and not licensed but stole the weapons and ammunition from his father's stash. How could he just up and leave the house one day with an AK 47 style rifle? Racquel couldn't get out of the house at the age of 20 with a dress too short!

How did this KID go undetected? Were there any signs? Did his other family members recognize his potential to become an active shooter and just ignored the warnings? How often did his Dad even check to make sure his guns and ammunition were as he had last left them? Was their leakage on Holtz's social media? Did he brag about what he wanted to do? Did he share with anyone? According to some of the reports Racquel read, there was usually some sort of leakage either on social media or with co-workers or friends prior to an active shooter event. Why didn't anyone report what they must have suspected about this kid! A disturbed youth with mass shooting potential.

If someone had just made one call to alert the authorities of Roy's threat potential. If someone had let them know that he had access to guns and didn't seem stable, then the authorities and trained personnel could have conducted their threat assessment and possibly prevented the deaths and injuries of dozens of people. It seemed simple enough. Report it and let the professionals figure it out. But no one reported anything about Roy Kenneth Holtz.

Holtz made plans that day as well, but it involved the sheer destruction of dozens of other people's plans, their lives and their future.

# CHAPTER TWENTY-THREE

**R**ACQUEL READ ABOUT THE OPTIONS established to assist someone involved in an active shooter event. One of the options was to engage the shooter in a fight. As Racquel sat in the family room all by herself, she said out loud, in total disgust, "Why the hell would I try to fight somebody with a gun?? That makes no damn sense!" Racquel heard the music turn down and her mom yell from the front office, "What did you say Roc?" She had been cursing more and more lately and recognized that she needed to get it under control quickly. "Nothing! I was talking to myself", Racquel replied.

Racquel had read the stories of regular citizens who did just that in so many instances, they risked their lives to stop gunmen. They fought back! They wrestled away jammed rifles, they retrieved their own weapons and shot back, they chased fleeing gunmen and shot them dead. Some people tackled gunmen and were killed. Others tackled gunmen and survived. Even at the mall on the day Racquel was involved in the mass shooting, a man picked up two chairs in the food court and hurled them at the gunman. His actions may have saved some other people from being shot and killed.

People were fighting back!! Racquel couldn't imagine having to do it herself but she knew that based on everything she had read, seen and heard, she better make plans on what to do if, God forbid, it were to happen again.

Racquel realized that it takes a special kind of person to fight back during an active shooter event. Some will run to save themselves and whomever they are with, others will hide in place and pray to God that the gunman doesn't find them and kill them or that the police will kill the gunman first, and yet others will fight back.

The guy who threw the chairs at the gunman, who was shot and injured, made plans for that day and he was determined not to let the gunman destroy his plans. He was a 34-year-old man, about 5 ft 10 in tall, medium build and still in relatively good shape but starting to get the over 30 belly bulge and jowl. His wife sent him out to the mall to pick up some last-minute items for her uncle and brother who were coming in to visit the next day.

He decided that, although his wife made and fed him a sandwich before he left for the mall, that he needed another bite to eat before he embarked on his shopping spree for manly gifts that only he could select. When the shooting began, he initially hid under the table where he had sat enjoying the food his wife would know nothing about.

Upon the realization that the table did not provide "cover" from the bullets, but only possibly kept him out of site, he decided to act. When he felt confident, he could make an impact, he jumped up and with each hand grabbed a chair and flung them at the gunman's back. The gunman's leg gave way and he stumbled back, but quickly recovered and immediately turned around and shot in his direction. The 34-year-old could not take cover quick enough and was grazed.

The funny part about this man's story, as Racquel found humor in everything, was that as he lay there bleeding, he thought about his family, friends, and his beautiful wife being mad that he was in the food court when she had given him a sandwich earlier. He could hear her saying to family and friends, "I don't even know why he was in the food court!" He thought about how mad she would be if he died right there in the food court because he was being greedy. He was determined not to die that day. And he did not!

## CHAPTER TWENTY-FOUR

**G**RADUATION DAY CAME IN MAY and Sydney and Raquel graduated. In four short years, they had done it! Mo was on an athletic 5-year program. Brandon needed at least one more year because of the transfer. Candice needed the fall semester before she would be able to graduate. In NY, Kelly (4 years) and Zeke (5 years) graduated. Zeke stayed in town and planned to attend NYU Law School. Kelly decided to get her Master's in Public Health and would consider Law school another time.

Sydney graduated with her bachelor's degree in Dance appreciation and planned to attend a graduate Program at the Mason Gross School of the Arts at Rutgers, The State University of New Jersey in New Brunswick, for her Master's in fine arts. Sydney was extremely excited about getting her first real apartment and heading to the area as a graduate student.

New Brunswick was just a short train ride from Newark, New Jersey and NY and was a 45 minute drive from Philadelphia. Sydney would have access to industry leaders in the area for teaching, training and working. She was also looking forward to a fresh start where people didn't know her history. She told Raquel and Candice that she was going to approach this chapter of her life

111

differently knowing that life is short and "You never know what the day holds." Racquel and Candice could certainly relate to that.

They all agreed to visit Jersey and check out the Rutgers New Brunswick campus. They had always heard mostly good things about Rutgers and looked forward to checking it out in the fall. Sydney was more a fan of basketball than football, so she recommended they join her for a basketball game. That way, it would not interfere with seeing Mo play in his last season of football.

One day, before the May graduation, Zeke called Racquel. He asked her how she was doing, how her leg felt. He inquired about how she and Mo were doing. Then Zeke told Racquel that now that Kelly was graduating, he wanted to propose to her. Since she and Racquel were best friends, he wanted her input on the style of the ring and what she might like.

Zeke made plans to meet up with Racquel. He drove to Racquel's campus and picked her up to shop for rings. He selected a beautiful 1 carat, princess cut diamond ring in a platinum setting that Racquel thought Kelly would be pleased with. He put a down payment on the ring and would pay it off over the summer.

He told Racquel of his plans to propose to Kelly in the fall and to do a better job at keeping the secret than she did at keeping she and Mo's relationship a secret. They laughed about that and Racquel promised not to say, text or breathe a word of it to Kelly or Mo.

Zeke returned Racquel to her campus and then headed to Kelly's parents' house with a picture of the ring, his intentions and to officially ask Kelly's Dad for her hand in marriage. "Real admirable, old school stuff right there" Racquel thought to herself, with a huge smile and significant approval. Zeke was a good man who checked off all of Kelly's boxes. He was almost too good to be true, but Racquel had seen him in action with her own eyes. She knew he was real and good and true.

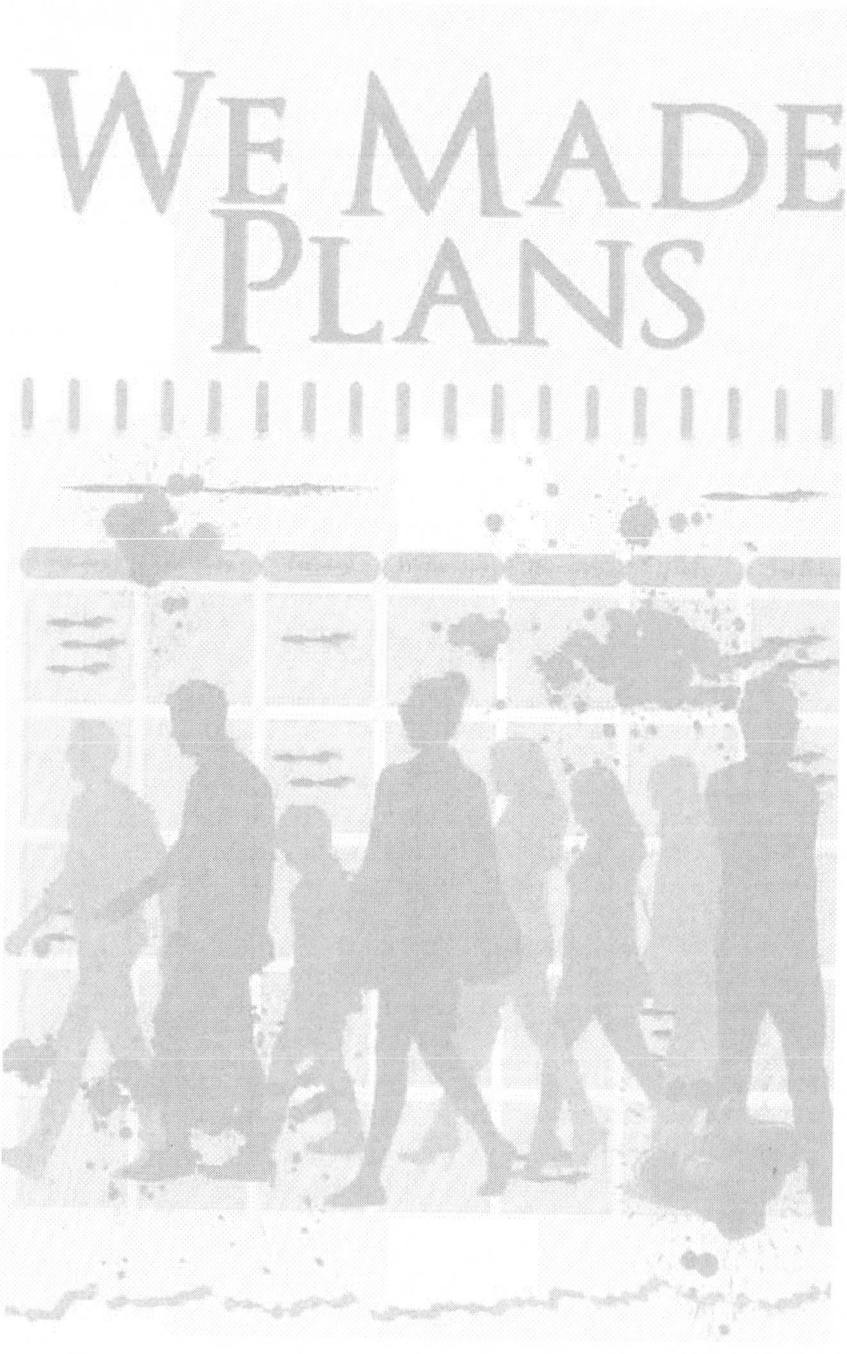
WE MADE
PLANS

# CHAPTER TWENTY-FIVE

RACQUEL MOVED BACK HOME after graduation which was something she didn't want to do when she left for college four years earlier. But now she wanted to be in the comfort of her home, surrounded by her loving family while she stacked her money to get her own place. Racquel wasn't happy about going back to her room or sharing a bathroom after having the luxury accommodations she had while in college. But it was a temporary solution toward a bigger, long-term goal, so she made the sacrifice.

One to two weekends a month, Racquel would visit Mo and stay the entire weekend. She also drove up to Rutgers to visit with Sydney. They went to a basketball game in the late fall on a Friday night and then headed over to the iconic Delta's Restaurant in downtown New Brunswick for dinner with Sydney's new boyfriend. He was a 25-year-old New Jersey State trooper who was born and raised in Jersey, East Orange, to be exact. He was proud to talk about his hometown where Lauryn Hill, Naughty by Nature, Althea Gibson, John Amos (Dad from Good Times) and Naturi Naughton (from Power) were all born and or raised. It was sort of cute to listen to his useless hometown facts that only really mattered to him and people from East Orange.

# We Made Plans

He could not make it in time for the Rutgers basketball game but wanted to make sure he made it to dinner. He paid for the entire meal and made sure they ate well. He didn't drink alcohol but ordered Racquel and Sydney whatever they wanted.

After dinner, Sydney demanded Racquel stay overnight and not drive back to Delaware. Racquel complied and slept on the comfy couch in the living room. She arose at about 8 am and made breakfast for she and Sydney. Then they headed out to check out some local sites.

Sydney enthusiastically showed Racquel the Mason Gross School of the Arts, The Zimmerli Art Museum, and the Crossroads Theater. She also referenced Charlotte from Sex in the City, Sheryl Lee Ralph and Paul Robeson. She was a beaming Rutgers connoisseur in just a few short months. Racquel was elated that Sydney was happy, almost giddy. She loved Sydney before, but she especially loved this happy, winning version of Sydney. She exuded a new-found confidence that Racquel hadn't noticed in undergrad. It was a marvelous thing.

She told Sydney how she felt because she learned that you have to say good things to and about people while they're living. Sydney smiled, hugged Racquel and said, "I'm happy and I'm trying girl, but thank you. I appreciate the love".

# CHAPTER TWENTY-SIX

**A**FTER MONTHS OF THE TORTURE OF RACQUEL keeping the secret, Zeke finally proposed to Kelly in the late fall. He hired a photography/videography team from upstate NY called Iron Visuals NY to capture the moments leading up to, during, and after the proposal in Times Square. The owner was a good friend from undergrad. All of Kelly's family drove out to NY Times Square but stayed out of site until the moment of the proposal.

Kelly and Zeke had a snack and lattes (drinking lattes was their thing). As they were crossing Time Square, Zeke pretended he forgot something at the coffee bar. At the sign of him tapping his pockets in the middle of Times Square, family and friends descended onto the square but still out of site. Zeke grabbed her hand to turn her around to follow him but then at the very center where the large tower of TVs looms overhead, Zeke abruptly stopped walking and reached into his pocket. He stood in front of Kelly holding her hand and then dropped down to one knee. Kelly placed her hand over her mouth and squealed with excitement, "What are you doing?" People with cell phones started to record the moment but the Iron Visuals NY team of 4 was able to distinguish themselves as the official videographer/photographers and bullied people out of the way to capture 360-degree rotations for video and excellent still shots.

Zeke began to tell Kelly of all the virtues he loved about her and that he wanted to spend the rest of his life with her. Then he held her left hand and slid a one carat princess cut diamond ring onto Kelly's ring finger and said, "Kelly, will you marry me?" Kelly jumped up and down, with tears streaming down her face and said, "yes, yes!" Zeke stood up, gently wiped her tears and gave her a huge kiss.

Then for video and picture purposes, in Racquel's humble opinion, he picked Kelly up and spun her around in the middle of Times Square. Family and friends joined them in Times Square as they moved off to the side. They then hailed yellow taxis to head to the Millicent Hotel for the engagement party dinner. Iron Visuals NY captured those moments as well. The finished video of the afternoon and evening's events would be shown at their late Spring wedding.

A late spring wedding meant that planning pretty much had to commence right away. Kelly asked Racquel to be her Maid of Honor the night of the proposal and engagement party and without hesitation, Racquel agreed. She would have been angry if Kelly had asked ANYONE else. Afterall, even Zeke understood their connection which is why Racquel was in on the ring selection. With that confirmation, Kelly asked two close cousins and two other friends from college to be her bride's maids. One half of the wedding party was complete!

They had a small private room at the Millicent and a DJ. They already set it up as if it were a wedding reception, but it was just the engagement party. They had appetizers as soon as they entered the room and a filling 3 course meal. They even had a sheet cake that said Congrats Ezekiel and Kelly with the date on it. "It was a good thing Kelly said yes", Racquel thought to herself and chuckled.

The attention to detail was an indication to Racquel that the actual wedding ceremony and reception was going to be spectacular. "Now, what does a Maid of Honor have to do exactly?" Racquel thought to herself and pulled out her phone to look it up. She typed in "Maid of honor esponsibilities". She looked at her entry, sucked her teeth and then deleted esponsibilities and typed in "responsibilities" so that it read "Maid of Honor responsibilities" and hit search. Several things popped up. Racquel sat back in the banquet chair and let the Maid of Honor training begin.

# CHAPTER TWENTY-SEVEN

**A**S THEY APPROACHED THE ONE-YEAR anniversary of the horrific mass shooting at the mall, two days before Christmas, they received requests for follow up interviews with the survivors and the families of those who lost their lives. It was horrible and Racquel wanted no part of the exploitation. She was trying to move on and didn't want anyone at her new job to know that she was a survivor of that horrific incident. Racquel declined each request.

Mo, on the other hand, thought it would be good for him to speak and do an interview. He thought it would be helpful to talk about it. He recounted the event from his perspective on three different occasions. They had agreed in advance not to mention Racquel directly but a persistent, rule breaking journalist, mentioned Racquel's name during the taping of the interview and said, "is that the person who was your girlfriend at the time?"

Mo was clearly irritated and stopped the interview. He said he specifically requested that her name not be used and that her privacy be respected. A Producer came over to calm him down and put in writing that no mention of Racquel by name would be included in the segment. He continued his recount of the events and that was the last interview he did.

# We Made Plans

The decision to go to NY for Christmas was never up in the air as much as it was approaching the 1-year anniversary following the mass shooting. Everyone was a little "gun shy". However, being a tenacious group, they would press on and not be defeated.

Kelly and Zeke were more comfortable in the hustle and bustle of NY than they were in the suburbs of Kelly's small town. They knew that NY was a potential target for almost everything like terror attacks, mass shootings, bombings, etc. but there was just something about New York that was comforting to them. They knew NY well. They didn't just reside there, they were living there and experiencing life as New Yorkers and were quite comfortable doing so. Kelly knew that she would never move back to Delaware and that NY was her new home.

December 20th Kelly and Zeke, Brandon and Candice, Mo and Racquel, and attending for the first time, Sydney and her State Trooper boyfriend, Will, visited NY for Christmas. They did some of their traditional yearly things but added new, quiet, more conservative and secure locations to their itinerary for the day. When the night was complete, without incident, they all were happy that they committed to going and thankful to be headed back home in one piece.

"Thank you, Lord", Racquel stated with a deep long sigh as she got in the car with Mo and buckled her seat belt. It was going to be a long ride home on the New Jersey Turnpike from the Jersey City train station to Delaware so she blasted the heat on her side of the car, put her jacket over her shoulders and neck, snuggled in and eventually drifted off to sleep. She awoke abruptly after a quick 20 minute cat nap. She knew Mo was tired too and she didn't feel right falling asleep on him while he had to make the drive home tired as well. It was better for both to be alert, rather than just the one.

# La Onque Chavette

At almost 2:30 am they arrived home. They sat in her driveway and talked for at least another half an hour. Mo was both excited and anxious about the professional league prospects. He spoke of a sports agent his Dad had been referred to and looked up. He talked about the Draft in the spring and how things move quickly once someone is drafted. There was talk of Mo being a late third early fourth round pick.

He really didn't want to go far away from his family but talked about that being the nature of the business. "You have to go to where they draft you and that's it" Mo said staring at the steering wheel. Racquel said to him, "That's OK Mo, we'll go wherever you need to be". It would be great if it were closer to home, but I'll take somewhere warm or wherever you need to go, really". She paused a moment. "I mean, I don't want to be presumptuous, do you even want me to go with you?" Racquel asked.

Mo looked at her in disgust and said, "Of course, I want you to go with me but you gotta stop saying dumb stuff!" Racquel laughed and said, "well I wasn't' sure what you were getting at". Mo said, "Yes Racquel, I want you to go with me. I need you to go with me! We'll be married like Zeke and Kelly soon enough but not before I'm drafted. You do want to marry me, right?" Racquel moved her head back slightly, raised her eyebrow and said hesitantly, "Is this an unofficial proposal?" Mo said, "It's a conversation and one that needs to be had because I don't want to propose to you in front of people and you say NO! I would be devastated." Racquel's lips turned down in a sad face and then she reached over and rubbed the back of his neck under his long thick dreadlocks.

She said, "Nope! I love you and I would never do that to you! When you ask me, I will say yes! Guaranteed!" Mo nodded

123

like he understood.  Then Racquel said in a low voice, "so you plan on proposing in front of a lot of people, huh?"  Mo laughed at Racquel and said, "Don't worry about it!  So nosey! Goodnight Roc!" and unlocked the car doors."

## CHAPTER TWENTY-EIGHT

**E**VERYONE MANAGED TO GET THROUGH the one-year anniversary of the mass shooting with the support of loving, caring, supportive and praying family members and friends. It was not easy at all. The memories of where you were exactly, what happened, how quickly it evolved, the sounds of complete chaos, tables & chairs screeching across the floors, drywall hitting the ground, people hitting the ground, the smells of the food court and the Chinese food place they were sitting across from, were seared into their minds.

They were literally sitting in the food court laughing at a stupid video. Racquel and Candice still could not remember the details of the video. That memory evaded them both. They were sitting there laughing and enjoying life, and in an instant, their lives changed forever.

It was the equivalent of using a ruler to draw a straight line down your last sheet of white paper when suddenly, the ruler moves, the pen jerks and your line shoots out a centimeter to the side. But you were using a pen so you can't erase it. You just try to realign the ruler and finish drawing the line. Maybe you can cover it up later or perhaps white it out or redact it but the mark is there, in pen, and unless you crumple up the paper and throw it out, you have to keep it and work around the jutted out pen mark.  It's a blemish on your paper.  This mass shooting they were involved in was more than just a blemish, however.  This event was a permanent, colossal, surgical scar and it altered the natural trajectory of their lives.

They all wafted through Christmas celebrations with barrages of calls, texts and e-mails from loved ones just checking on their state of mind during the anniversary of the mass shooting. Their families thought it was necessary to check on their mental health and to make sure they were addressing the trauma of the event effectively.  "I'm ok", Racquel would say.  "I'm fine and so is Racquel", Mo would say.  They appreciated the love.

New Year celebrations, the Superbowl, Valentine's Day, a football Combine invite and Easter were celebrated with the usual hoopla and no problems.  Everyone kind of hurried through mindlessly, almost floating through the holidays and special events. Now the time had come for Mo's draft day followed by Kelly and Zeke's wedding.

They were the two most important events of the season. Racquel felt overwhelmed at times trying to juggle the planning of the Bridal shower and the stresses of Mo's draft day preparation.  He was training in different states, traveling for meetings and workouts. He literally traversed the country.  He worked out in Arizona, Florida, Massachusetts, Pennsylvania, New York, Minnesota, and Kansas.

His family was planning a draft day party at his home on the Saturday of the Draft weekend which would be the day the third and fourth rounders would be drafted.  They weren't doing anything "too big" because Mo was so anxious.  For Mo's family, "Nothing too big" meant just 30-40 of his closest family members, good friends, former coaches and some others that Racquel had never met in all the years that she had known Mo (9 years). Of course, Mo's doting mom, who loved to cook, prepared a smorgasbord of food reminiscent of Thanksgiving Dinner and Superbowl Sunday combined.

She had a whole, nicely browned turkey with the legs still perfectly pinned together at the knees as opposed to gaped open, like a cheap ho, sausage stuffing, string beans, seafood salad, homemade subs, fried chicken, especially tender beef brisket, garlic parmesan wings, and buffalo wings with blue cheese dressing, chili cheese dip, and spinach dip.

She served 2 different green salads, and towards the end of the night put out several different desserts including red velvet cake, apple pie, chocolate walnut brownies, cannolis, Italian rum cake, and a triple chocolate cake. Not to mention the chocolate chip cookies and chips that were out all day. She also set up the Keurig for coffee or hot chocolate to compliment the desserts. Racquel and Mo didn't know how she managed everything, but she did it and did it well! She kept everyone fed all day long.

Midafternoon Mo's cell phone rang. He yelled, "I'm getting a call! Quiet!!" One aunt screamed as if she were startled by an intruder before her husband covered her mouth with his hand. Everyone said SHHHHH! far longer than necessary and Mo waved his hand to be quiet. Everyone finally settled down as Mo said, "Hello". His mom grabbed Racquel's hand and moved her in to stand right next to Mo with his Dad on the other side. Mo started smiling as they could hear a deep voice in the distance saying something to Mo. "Yes Sir", Mo said. "Absolutely... oh no doubt,

127

Sir." Mo said. "Absolutely", Mo stated as his eyes filled up with tears. "Yes, Sir and thank you so much. Thank you. I will not disappoint! ... yes, uh huh, I'm looking forward to it" Mo said and hung up the phone. Mo didn't say a word. No one saw the area code so while they knew Mo was officially drafted. They had no idea where. Mo hugged his mom and dad and cried.

One of his Uncle's yelled, "Where you goin boy??" An aunt yelled, "Mo if you don't tell us who was on that phone..." Racquel looked at Mo and had absolutely no idea who called him. He was entangled in an embrace with his Mom and Dad, but he glanced down at the remote. Racquel saw his teary almost hazel eyes and grabbed the remote and turned the TV up as loud as necessary to drown out the noise of the family yelling and threatening Mo. Mo pulled Racquel toward him, held her tight and kissed her on the side of her neck. His tears rolled down her neck to the top of her shoulder just as it was announced, "with the 124$^{th}$ pick of the NFL Draft, the Philadelphia Eagles select Morton Thomas Goodwin."

The whole house erupted in cheers. They must have been heard the next block over. They were jumping up and down, yelling, screaming, high fiving each other, running around the room like they had the Holy Ghost. They were hugging each other and totally on top of the world. "Morton Thomas Goodwin, my Mo, was drafted to the Philadelphia Eagles." Racquel thought to herself amid all the celebration. She hugged and kissed Mo and moved out of the way so that the host of shouting family, friends and coaches could congratulate him. She was confident that she would have more time with him later that night.

Racquel's phone started to vibrate with buzzing from several text messages.

"Roc tell Mo I said Congrats!!"

"Hey Racquel, I'm so happy for you and Mo.  Give him a kiss for me and tell him congrats!!"  Kelly and Zeke

"Congrats to Mo!"

"Go head Mo!"

"The Eagles suck but congrats to Mo!"

"Hey Raquel, we going to the EAGLE's games oh yeah, oh yeah, LOL  Tell Mo congrats!"  Candice

"Woo hoooo!!! Congrats to Mo, you know I want 2 tickets to a game.  Thanks cuz"

"MOOOOOOOOOOO!  Racquel that is awesome!  I'm going to be an Eagles fan now even though I don't like football.  Tell Mo congrats!"  HS classmate

"Heyyyy Racquel!  Congrats to Mo and to you for picking a winner!!"  Sydney

Endless text messages from family and friends were received that evening.  Everyone was either extremely happy for Mo or put in their bid for tickets early.  Brandon came over to Racquel to tell her about the text messages he received with instructions to congratulate Mo.  They compared notes on how many asked for tickets and laughed about it.  Brandon said, "Mo is going to need someone to screen these new fake friends for him.  Racquel said, "Nah, I think he's pretty set on who his friends are and that's us! NO NEW FRIENDS!" and they both laughed.

129

When the dust settled, after neighbors and friends streamed in to touch Mo and put their hands on a future professional league player, and all the family, including Racquel's family, and friends left, Mo and Racquel had a chance to sit, hug and talk. Racquel congratulated him and talked about his hard work paying off and how excited she was for him. Mo said, "Racquel be excited for us! This is OUR new journey! Stop being like that. I've been exclusively yours for a long time and wanted this for you as much as I have wanted it for my parents and family. We all gonna be elevated with this. So, stop being modest and acknowledge that ya man is going to be an NFL player!!" They laughed, hugged and kissed for a long time.

# CHAPTER TWENTY-NINE

**O**N A GORGEOUS SATURDAY AFTERNOON in June, with a clear blue sky and 77-degree temperatures, Racquel and 200 other family, friends, colleagues and loved ones streamed into the Ebenezer Baptist Church in Jamisville, Delaware, where Kelly's family had been long time members. The Pastor, Reverend Mitchell, knew Kelly from when she was in the 6th grade. He had watched her blossom into a gorgeous young lady with a biblical, virtuous woman like demeanor and he was honored for the opportunity to marry her off to such a God fearing, humble provider, and young man as Zeke.

There was no doubt in Pastor Mitchell's mind that Zeke would be able to lead and be the head of the household while loving Kelly as Jesus loves the church. He went on and on about how great they were and while Racquel knew it, she was tired of listening to the Pastor because the balls of her feet were starting to feel numb in her heels and she had a long day ahead with all her Maid of Honor responsibilities. She preferred not to walk around with achy feet.

Racquel had to be patient and suck it up as the ceremony lasted for 45 minutes. Then they had to stand in line to shake hands with everyone on the way out.

# We Made Plans

The entryway of the Church was grand. Two steps and a 30 foot walkway led to 12-foot wooden double doors with oversized black iron handles. The Foyer had at least a 24-foot ceiling. The floors were covered in subtle red carpet. The center aisle was designed for weddings and the choirs march. Each side of the center aisle was flanked with two columns of rows of pews.

There were grand chandeliers over the center of each of the four columns of rows and additional chandeliers above the pulpit and choir area. The church held 600 members and guests comfortably. There was also several choir rehearsal rooms, a nursery, a gym, administrative and minister's offices and a huge kitchen for church catered events.

Zeke and Kelly decided to only have the wedding ceremony at Kelly's hometown church. The reception was held at the Delaware Blu Grand Solarium and Ballroom. A private, elaborate location about 25 minutes away from the church. The entry was off a quiet side road where you entered in through the huge iron gates to a tree lined, scenic, ½ mile path that led to a circular drive where you exited the car for valet parking. Every guest was greeted at the door with hot towels to clean their hands and then directed to waiters with glasses of champagne. Just beyond the entryway, to the right, was a gorgeous garden room with a variety of heavily scented, vividly hued flowers, floral arrangements in assorted vases, and bench seats in front of six-foot tiered fountains and 1-2-foot trickling fountains, all strategically placed throughout the garden. There were sitting areas under pergolas surrounded by well-manicured evergreens. It was the perfect place for taking pictures and everyone took lots of them.

Everyone exited through a 12-foot-high, retractable glass door to the right of the garden room into a grand ballroom with floor to ceiling windows that overlooked a mini English garden. A baby grand piano was set in the back left of the ballroom. An extremely talented pianist played for an hour straight while everyone dined on appetizers and enjoyed the open bar. But aha!! Kelly's Christian family only allowed the open bar to serve select wines, water and non-alcoholic beverages. Mo and Racquel laughed so hard at that realization. Mo said, "We're definitely serving real liquor at our reception." "Right" Racquel declared as she sipped her wine and they both laughed about it.

There was a 10-foot round, 6-foot-high table in the center of the room with a full assortment of salmon and other fish, bruschetta, fruits, veggies, assorted cheeses and crackers, shrimp, baby lamb chops, Swedish meatballs, leafy green salads and more. There were about 20 assorted pub style and banquet style tables and stools placed sporadically throughout the ball room for guests to enjoy as they dined.

After a little less than an hour of enjoying their time in the grand ballroom, guests were directed to an even bigger, more lavish ballroom than the first one, called the Grand Ballroom Blu. This ballroom looked out onto a man-made lake with several water fountains spouting water about 20 feet high. Later in the evening, the fountains would be well illuminated.

Back inside the Grand Ballroom Blu, there was a tall fireplace with an intricately detailed mantel sitting about 8 feet high, topped with a 6 foot mirror tilted back to reflect the light from the excessive number of grand, warmly lit, chandeliers, and floor to ceiling windows with long embroidered silver drapes. The round banquet tables sat 10 people each and were draped with white and sparkly silver tablecloths. Each centerpiece towered 4 feet high above the table and was capped off with magnificent floral arrangements.

The wedding party was set at a long rectangular glass table with the Bride and Groom at center. Four tall glass vases illuminated by pink neon lights at the base were placed along the front of the table. A compliment of pink and silver place settings marked the spot for each member of the wedding party.

The Grand Ballroom Blu housed the DJ and he wasn't allowed to play one single thing until the first guests entered the room. He then had to start with light jazz music until all guests were out of the first ballroom. Then and only then was he allowed to start the music with Kool and the Gang's "Let's Celebrate". That was Kelly and Zeke's parents' idea of getting the party started right. People partied, danced, snapped pictures and ate another 5-course meal before the night was out. Zeke and Kelly danced to all the edited versions of the music that Kelly's parents allowed them to play.

The music was great actually and Kelly seemed to be having a great time. She also looked absolutely gorgeous!! Zeke didn't look too bad himself. Before the night was out, Racquel demanded the photographer take a picture of her, Kelly, Zeke, Mo, Brandon and Candice. Then they got rid of Candice and Zeke and just took a picture of the four of them. Brandon, Mo, Kelly and Racquel. That was it. Just the four of them.

That would be the last time they'd kick spouses out of a picture because Zeke wasn't going to allow it again. They knew this because he specifically said it to Racquel. Candice chimed in with, "Yeah Racquel!!," in support of Zeke's statement.

Brandon looked at his good friend Kelly smiling and said, "You look beautiful Mrs. Ellington. I'm so happy for you" He then gave her a big hug and a kiss on her cheek. Kelly returned the hug and said, "I love you Brandon". He said, "I love you too Kels". "So, you and Candice up next?" Kelly inquired.

Brandon looked at her and said, "before Mo and Roc?? I don't know about that one." Kelly scanned the room for Mo and Racquel and said, "Yeah they probably will be next, but this is not a race or a competition Brandon. If you love someone, why wait? Brandon looked at Kelly and said, "Yes, I know, I know but this is your night, stop trying to marry me off too!"

The DJ played Maxwell's "Fortunate" and Mo ran over to find Racquel. He said, 'Hey gorgeous, Can you take off 5 minutes from your Maid of Honor duties to dance with me?" "Of course, I can" Racquel said with an alluring smile. Then she put her arms around his neck, and they slow danced. Raquel rested her head on Mo's chest, took a deep breath and a long sigh. Racquel felt safe and comfortable in Mo's arms. She closed her eyes and enjoyed the moment.

Mo, being Mo, interrupted the moment with an attempt to sing. "I'm fortunate to have you girl, I'm so glad you're in my world, Just as sure as the sky is blue, I'm blessed the day that I found you".

Racquel laughed at his vulnerability in attempting to sing any Maxwell song. It didn't really matter because at that moment, she didn't want to be wrapped up in anyone else's arms tolerating the pitchiness. "Mo" Racquel said. "Yes" Mo replied. "You have a nice voice babe" Racquel said snickering. Mo pushed her arms-length away laughing and said, "so now you just gonna start lying?".

"Racquel Amani Wilson don't lie to me" Then he pulled her back in and kept dancing and singing. "I'm so mighty mighty proud about it, no shame in my gaaaame, ooooohhhhhhh" as they rocked back and forth.

# CHAPTER THIRTY

**M**R. EZEKIEL SAMUEL ELLINGTON AND Mrs. Kelly H.(still can't ask her about her middle name) Ellington sent thank you cards out to their guests within two weeks of their return from their honeymoon. The thank you cards were just as elaborate as the proposal, invitations, ceremony and reception. Their parents spared no expense.

Kelly checked in with Racquel upon her return. Racquel's cell phone rang and it was Kelly on the other line. Racquel picked up and said "Heeeeyyyyy Kelly or should I say Mrs. Ellington. How you doin?" "Hey Roc! I'm good. I just wanted to let you know I'm back in town. How are you doing?" Kelly said. "I'm good, thanks. Soooo tell me about the honeymoon. How was Italy?" Racquel inquired. Once given the green light, Kelly and Racquel talked for 45 minutes about all things Italy and Zeke.

Racquel said, "So when are you going to make me an auntie?" Kelly said, "funny you should ask me that..." Racquel screamed in Kelly's ear and then she said, "You're pregnant? Oh my God Kelly!" Kelly laughed and laughed and said, "No, no, no, not yet, but I wanted to hear your reaction" "We're not ready to have kids just yet, but eventually."

# We Made Plans

"Kelly how are you going to let me get excited about it and then burst my bubble?" Racquel said. Kelly said, "you started blowing the bubble with Bubble Yum bubble gum, there was no stopping it" and laughed. Racquel said, "OK bye Kelly". "Byyyyeeee Roc" Kelly said laughing as they hung up.

# CHAPTER THIRTY-ONE

**I**N MID JULY MO WAS PREPARING TO REPORT TO another camp for the Philadelphia Eagles. There were some 99- degree temps in the days leading up to the first day of camp where all the veterans would be present. By the first day though, the temperatures were back down to the mid 80s which was a relief, by comparison.

Mo spent a great deal of time studying the playbook and going through the grueling practices. Mo was extremely competitive, and he was working hard to show off his skills. This opportunity was something he had waited his whole life for, and he was not going to blow it. He was coachable and worked well with all the position coaches. He was also fun to be around, so he genuinely got along well with his teammates.

Mo was there as a rookie and the veterans were sure to treat him as a rookie in terms of carrying equipment, buying his position mates water ice and Popeyes chicken and making him sing during karaoke night. He had fun and took it all in stride. But his focus was to learn the playbook, handle his business on and off the field and to bond with his teammates; to develop that camaraderie that you always hear about with football players.

# We Made Plans

Raquel, Brandon, Candice, Kelly, Zeke, Sydney and Will made plans to go to the last pre-season game where Mo would probably get a good amount of game time experience. Brandon was always an Eagles fan and already had several jerseys, like Brian Dawkins, Donovan McNabb, and Desean Jackson's. Racquel and Kelly wore their new Eagles' jerseys.

Sydney, who didn't even like football was now a Giants fan thanks to her Jersey born, north Jersey living, State Trooper boyfriend, Will. He was respectful and wore a simple black fitted shirt with jeans. But he absolutely would NOT don an Eagles jersey for anyone! No way, not even for Mo, his girlfriend's best friend's boyfriend, who gave him a free ticket.

They enjoyed the atmosphere of the pre-season game. They sang the Fly Eagles Fly fight song and Racquel tried her best to enjoy the moment and not think about the possibility of an active shooter event at the game. Afterall, they diligently checked her bag and everyone else's. They even had to go through metal detectors. So, there was no need to worry about anything.

Racquel's mind wouldn't let her rest. Mo was on the field so if anything went down, she would have to take care of herself. Racquel made sure to look at the different exits, the nearest exits, places where she could take cover or hide. She leaned over to Candice and said, "take note of the exits Candice". Candice didn't turn her head, she kept her eyes fixed on the field and said, "Oh I already checked for that. I'm two steps ahead of you, but thanks."

Then, she grabbed Racquel's hand and squeezed it. She said, "aaaahh, we're going to be OK but it's good to be alert." Kelly heard the conversation and scooched over to put her arm around Racquel and Candice. Then she said, "God's got us. There's no need

140

to be fearful. He's got us!" Candice said, "Amen" and Racquel said, "Amen to that!" Racquel remembered that she, indeed, had the best friends ever.

# CHAPTER THIRTY-TWO

**P**RESEASON WAS OVER, THE BUZZ ABOUT MO was on. He performed well enough to hope to see some game time this year! Mo was hyped up about the buzz he had heard but he tried to remind himself not to get caught up with what he was hearing because, in this business, just as quickly as they learn to love you, they start to hate you, especially in Philly. Passionate fans lived in Philly, South Jersey and Delaware and Mo remembered how he, himself, turned on a few players in his lifetime when they started to mess up. Therefore, Mo tried to remain level-headed about the brotherly love.

Racquel was at her house cleaning the kitchen when she started to feel a little lightheaded. Her mom made her sit down and brought her a glass of water. Not knowing what was wrong, her mom started in with the, "I told you to drink more water Roc and to stay hydrated. It's still too hot outside! How many bottles of water did you have today?"

Her Mom was about to start on the 6th or 7th statement/question when Racquel bolted up out of the seat and sprinted over to the garbage can to vomit. "Oh Lord, what did you eat Racquel?" Racquel had only eaten some hotdogs and French fries, nothing unusual. It should not have made her feel sick, especially not sick enough to vomit. Racquel wasn't the vomiting type. She could hold her own in everything. Racquel said to her Mom, "I don't know what I ate", then she went to her room to lie down.

Racquel's cell phone buzzed and a picture of Mo smiling and shirtless popped up. His cell phone name was "Love of my life". Racquel answered the phone and said, "Hi Mo." Mo asked her how she was doing, and she told him that she just vomited and didn't feel good. Racquel blamed it on the stadium hotdogs and vowed not to eat them again. Mo agreed that she should stay away from the stadium hotdogs.

Mo called her because he wanted to take Racquel out to dinner. He gave specific instructions to dress nice, make sure her hair was done and her makeup on. Racquel thought for sure a proposal was on its way because he said after he was drafted. He would propose after he was drafted. Maybe he was ready to officially and finally make it happen.

They made plans to meet for dinner in Philly the next night. Just the two of them. No teammates, no family, no friends. Just the two of them, so he said.

Racquel was not feeling well but she put on her best face, long fitted black dress, to cover the scar on her calf, and Eagles green pumps with accessories. She had her hair done at the salon earlier in the day, so she was pulled together. If this was the proposal and it was going to be recorded, she had to look her best and she was ready.

On the way up to Philly, Racquel started to feel nauseous again. So much so that she had to pull over on 95 so that she could vomit. She grabbed a plastic Wawa bag filled with old Wawa

French vanilla coffee cups. When she was done her eyes were bloodshot red and she had vomit breath. "Ughhhhahhh!" She moaned. She stopped at Walgreens and picked up a travel size mouthwash, a pack of gum, and some other items. She fixed her face, rinsed and spit the mouthwash, then popped three pieces of gum in her mouth.

Mo was already parked so he told her to meet him at the front of the restaurant and he would ride with her to find a place to park. Racquel was very alert the whole night; but not looking for a potential active shooter, she was looking for camera guys or family members who didn't know how to stay out of sight.

The whole night it was just Mo and Racquel. No surprise proposal. But knowing Mo, he was probably trying to set her up because he knew that she was nosey and would expect a proposal then. He would want it to be a surprise. Racquel wanted Mo to ask on his own when he was ready. She just hoped he would do so sooner rather than later.

# CHAPTER THIRTY-THREE

**R**ACQUEL TOOK ADVANTAGE OF THE TIME away from Mo while he was in camp to immerse herself in other productive activities. She picked up a couple of books from the local bookstore and read them intensely. "Discovering Your Divine Natural Abilities; A book on self-discovery, chasing after dreams and the comfort of finding out who you really are" written by Jeanetta Thomas and "I'm Still Here; From Heart Failure to Heart of a Champion" written by Johnnie Davis.

Racquel was truly inspired by these two extraordinary books. She jotted down notes, highlighted paragraphs and turned down pages in both books. Racquel felt a new awakening and contemplated her own story and purpose. Something was brewing.

A couple of weeks into training camp, Racquel's phone buzzed for a face to face call and it was "Love of my life" calling. "Racquel fixed her hair, propped the phone in the holder at a perfect angle for a face to face call and picked up. "Hi Mo" she said in a sweet voice. Mo asked how she was doing. Racquel took a deep breath in and blew out a long sigh. "What's wrong?" Mo asked. Racquel said, "Mo remember the night of Kelly and Zeke's wedding" before you left for rookie camp...?" Mo smiled approvingly, reached over, patted his own back and said, "yeah and apparently so do you." and laughed a dirty, perverted laugh.

Racquel just stared at the phone and Mo stopped laughing abruptly. With a concerned look on his face, he began a barrage of questions starting with, "Why Roc? Why are you asking me if I remember that night? What's wrong with you because I know... Are you...?" Racquel interrupted Mo and said, "I was inspired by our conversation that night." Mo looked perplexed and in a curious voice he inquired, "inspired by something I SAID??"

"Yes Mo. Inspired by something you SAID!" Racquel emphasized.

Mo said. "OK so what did I say that has you all worked up...again" and belted out another dirty, perverted laugh. Racquel stared at that phone and tried not to laugh but she couldn't hold it in. She burst into laughter dropping her head down and knocking over the phone. She picked up the phone, repositioned it and continued the conversation. "Mo, I need you to be serious and hear me out". He sat up straight and in an annoyed voice, he demanded, "Roc what is it, say it already!"

Racquel said, "I need to know your thoughts on this because what I'm about to tell you will affect our future and you as a football player." Mo hesitantly said, "OK" swallowed hard and waited for Racquel to proceed. Racquel gathered her thoughts and slowly began, "I'm a social media management consultant and I've enjoyed what I've been doing since graduation. I've learned a great deal through my internship and my current job. I'm not quitting my job or anything but I'm going to spend time managing my own social media." Mo hesitantly said, "OK" Racquel went on to say, "I've been doing a lot of research about active shooters, mass shootings and how to survive a mass shooting. Not everyone will have a knight in shining armor, like yourself, to whisk them away from danger. "

"People need to know what to do and how to do it. Split second decisions must be made because every second counts. Women need to feel empowered to fight back, AS A LAST RESORT, of course, but fight back nonetheless" Racquel emphasized. "Women need to feel empowered and they need to hear this from a woman's perspective. So, I'm going to start by using my social media platforms to inform people and then I'm going to move into speaking engagements and workshops. So how does this affect you? If you plan on having a future with me…"

Mo took an annoyed deep breath and threw both hands in the air. He was about to interrupt Racquel, but she continued in a louder voice, "IT's POSSIBLE THAT MYYYYYY…" When Mo settled down, Racquel lowered her voice again and said, "It's possible that my discussing and teaching on this topic may bring unwanted attention and what I do in the public eye may affect you directly or indirectly. If you think this is going to be a problem for you, then I can maybe use an alias or something. It may be better to use an alias anyway. I'm not sure." Racquel blew out a deep breath and sigh of relief and then she asked, "So, what do you think?"

Mo smiled and said, "I think it's an excellent idea, but you can't use an alias because you already have a significant following with your name. I don't think you should start from scratch with that. I think you've become quietly passionate about this since it happened to us and I think you should share with the world. You would be great at it!! Don't worry about me and how it will affect me. We'll be ok. I think you should go for it!" Racquel smiled approvingly and said, "Thanks Mo. I am passionate about this. People need to know, and this is the way I think I can make a positive impact." Mo agreed and encouraged Racquel to make plans to get started.

Racquel discussed with her parents and family who would also be impacted by her decision and they were happy for her. Her Dad thought it would be great for her mental health and stability to pursue her idea. Racquel finally shared with Brandon, Kelly, Candice and Sydney, her best friends and, next to Mo, most supportive friends ever. They were excited for Racquel and were happy for her decision. Kelly, Sydney and Candice said they would use their connections to try to arrange a few speaking engagements.

Racquel prepared a PowerPoint presentation and made her family provide real feedback. If they didn't understand something, she wanted to know. If the sentences didn't flow smoothly, she wanted to know. How did they feel after sitting through her presentation? Were they more informed than before? What was she missing from her presentation? How were the graphics she chose, the sound effects, etc. They were given a specific set of instructions to think about as they sat through her presentations and the revisions of her presentations. She studied her notebook and made changes to her social media profiles to reflect that she was available for speaking engagements. Then, she jotted down draft ideas for her first few postings. A few weeks after her facetime conversation with Mo, Racquel made plans to start her new business passion. She typed out her first post and sent it on all her social media platforms. It read,

"My name is Racquel Amani Wilson. My friends and family call me Roc and I'm a SURVIVOR of the Delaware Mall Christmas mass shooting. My objective is to help someone avoid and/or

150

survive a mass shooting by becoming more knowledgeable and empowered to do something, whether it's to hide or run or attack. Let's talk about your plans!"

# AUTHOR'S NOTES

**W**E **MADE PLANS** is a fictional story that intertwines the harsh reality of active shooter events in the United States of America. The author attempts to develop the characters and their relationships with one another lulling the reader with intricate details in anticipation of what happens next in their lives, individually and collectively. As real life would have it, things can change in an instant and they did for this group of friends.

Being unprepared for such an event, it was important for Racquel to discover how to prepare going forward. Racquel's character wanted others to be proactive and deliberate in giving thought to what to do in the event one is ever involved in an active shooter situation. Racquel's post mass shooting response was designed to make one think about his/her surroundings, take note of people in their presence, and determine exit strategy options.

It's not something to be consumed with daily, but it is something to give, at the very least, a fleeting thought. Look for those exit signs! What object can provide cover to slow down or prevent the penetration of bullets? Where in the office, mall, building or place of employment can you hide if necessary. What everyday item such as a chair, scissors or steaming pot of hot coffee, can serve as a weapon against an active shooter.

Give serious thought to the options of RUN HIDE FIGHT. If possible, distance yourself from the active shooter quickly. In other words, GET OUT OF THERE! Hide in a location where you can't easily be seen. Think back to your days of playing Hide n' Go Seek. Avoid hiding in an unlockable location where there's only one way in and one way out, as in a bathroom. If you must hide, lock yourself in if you can, turn off your cell phone volume, and turn off lights.

Fight, ONLY AS A LAST RESORT, and because your life and the plans you made with those you love, depend on it. To fight is more akin to an attack on the gunman. While it's always better to do this as a group, if by yourself, be deliberate and relentless in your attack. No holds barred. In fact, no matter who is with you, be relentless in attacking and disarming the gunman.

If you suspect someone of having the potential to commit such a heinous crime, please take the tough step to report them. This may prove difficult because the person may be a co-worker, a family member, a fellow student, or your best friend since kindergarten. Your decision to make a call to report, or to send a referral could save several lives, maybe even hundreds of lives.

The impact of an active shooter event effects far more than the direct victims of the event. Family members are devastated over the loss and or must learn to cope with the injuries their loved one sustained. Co-workers are traumatized and the nation is struck with fear, anger and despair. If it is determined that the person is not a threat, that's great! But if you choose not to say or do anything and that person takes the opportunity to commit a mass murder, then that will be on your mind forever. Basically, if you strongly suspect, or have a gut feeling, or have heard the potential shooter say, write or post something, please trust your gut and say something to a teacher, a manager, a family member or the authorities. Let the professionals figure it out.

# We Made Plans

People make plans daily, unaware of, and oblivious to the fact that things change unexpectedly and in an instant. While finishing up the book, We Made Plans, two active shooter events occurred within less than 24 hours of each other in El Paso, Texas and Dayton, Ohio, in the United States. To say that active shooter events have been on a disturbing and upward trend is an understatement.

Be safe, be vigilant and be blessed.

## Active Shooter Incidents in the United States in 2018

US Department of Justice, Federal Bureau of Investigation Report

* "The FBI defines an active shooter as one or more individuals actively engaged in killing or attempting to kill people in a populated area. Implicit in this definition is the shooter's use of one or more firearms. The active aspect of the definition inherently implies that both law enforcement personnel and citizens have the potential to affect the outcome of the event based upon their responses to the situation."

Report based on 27 FBI defined incidents

"Citizen Engagement and Casualties

In five incidents, citizens confronted the shooter.

In three incidents, unarmed citizens confronted the shooter, thereby ending the shooting

- In one incident, (Waffle House Shooting) a citizen wrestled the gun away from the shooter…
- In one incident, (Hot Yoga Tallahassee Shooting) citizens confronted the shooter (including one who was pistol-whipped by the shooter) allowing others to flee the scene…
- In one incident, (Noblesville Middle School Shooting) a teacher wrestled the shooter to the ground and restrained him until law enforcement arrived…

# We Made Plans

In two incidents, (Louie's Lakeside Eatery and Kroger Grocery Store) armed citizens possessing valid firearm permits exchanged gunfire with the shooter

- In one incident, two citizens retrieved their guns from their respective vehicles, then shot and killed the shooter.
- In one incident, a citizen armed with a gun confronted the shooter, but no gunfire was exchanged. A second citizen exchanged gunfire with the shooter, but neither was struck…

## The Shooters (Based on 27 FBI defined incidents)

Twenty-three shooters were male; three shooters were female.

The shooters ranged in age from 13 to 64 years

11 shooters were apprehended by law enforcement

5 shooters were killed

10 shooters committed suicide

1 shooter still at large

## Locations

16 of the 27 incidents occurred in areas of commerce

5 of the 27 occurred in education environments

2 of the 27 occurred in open space

2 of the 27 occurred in health care facilities

1 of the 27 occurred on government property

1 of the 27 occurred in a house of worship

**As in past years, Citizens were faced with split second, life and death decisions. In 2018, citizens risked their lives to safely and successfully end the shootings in five of the 27 active shooter incidents. They saved many lives. Given this reality, it is vital that citizens be afforded training, so they understand the risks they face and the options they have available when active shooter incidents are unfolding.**

Likewise, law enforcement must remain vigilant regarding prevention efforts and aggressively train to better respond to – and help communities recover from – active shooter incidents. The FBI remains committed to assisting state, local, tribal, and campus law enforcement in its active shooter prevention, response, and recovery efforts"

## References and Links

Active Shooter Incidents in the United States in 2018
U.S. Department of Justice, Federal Bureau of Investigations

https://www.fbi.gov/file-repository/active-shooterincidents-in-the-us-2018-041019.pdf/view

A Study of the Pre-Attack Behaviors of Active Shooters in the United States Between 2000 and 2013
U.S. Department of Justice, Federal Bureau of Investigations

https://www.fbi.gov/file-repository/pre-attack-behaviorsof-active-shooters-in-us-2000-2013.pdf/view

FBI Active Shooter Resources

https://www.fbi.gov/about/partnerships/office-of-partnerengagement/active-shooter-resources

National Threat Assessment Center

https://www.secretservice.gov/protection/ntac/

Run Hide Fight: Surviving an Active Shooter Event Video

https://youtu.be/5VcSwejU2D0 Echoes of Columbine

Video https://youtu.be/zgeRtRo862w


National Threat Assessment Center (2019). Mass Attacks in Public Spaces - 2018. U.S. Secret Service, Department of Homeland Security https://www.secretservice.gov/data/press/reports/US SS_FY2019_MAPS.pdf

Lessons from a Workplace Shooting in Virginia Beach

https://worldview.stratfor.com/article/lessons-workplaceshooting-virginia-beach

Article - The U.S. Once had a Ban on Assault Weapons – Why Did It Expire   NPR.org August 13, 2019

https://www.npr.org/2019/08/13/750656174/the-u-s-oncehad-a-ban-on-assault-weapons-why-did-it-expire

STOP THE BLEED  SAVE A LIFE  Bleeding Control

https://www.bleedingcontrol.org/

Text to 911

https://www.fcc.gov/consumers/guides/text-911-quick-

facts-faqs https://www.wikihow.com/Text-911

https://www.apnews.com/93b9cf8a789b4a5ea32105d7f2

eb6aa7 https://www.tech.nj.gov/911/


Iron Visuals NY www.ironvisuals.com

Discovering your Divine Natural Abilities by Jeanetta Thomas
https://www.amazon.com/Discovering-your-DIVINE-NATURAL-ABILITIES/dp/1688281975

I'm still Here: From Heart Failure to Heart of a Champion by Johnnie Davis

https://m.barnesandnoble.com/w/im-still-here-johnnie-davis/1126452893?ean=9780692872338

Zimmerli Art Museum at Rutgers

http://www.zimmerlimuseum.rutgers.edu/

Delta's Southern Cuisine and Cocktails

http://www.deltasrestaurant.com/

Crossroads Theatre Company

http://www.crossroadstheatrecompany.org/

# ACKNOWLEDGEMENT

I would like to first and foremost thank my Lord and Savior, Jesus Christ! The idea, inspiration and mindset to write and complete this book is all thanks to God. Next, I want to thank my ever supportive, patient, loving, praying, handsome husband who allowed me the time to cocoon and write for hours and days. I thank you for everything! Thanks to my wonderful, beautiful, intelligent children who have contributed in innumerable ways to my success.

To my sister and niece, thank you for all that you've done each time I sent a text asking/demanding you read this and review that. I am thankful for your input and grateful to have you!

To all of my extended family, friends and colleagues who've supported, encouraged and motivated me throughout this process, thank you so much! Love you all!

The push I needed to get this work published came from witnessing a long-time friend, and now author, see her own work through to fruition. She willingly and generously shared with me and I am forever grateful to her! Thank you, J!

Thank you to my very straight forward publisher who had to yank the manuscript from me and say, "Let's do this!". Thank you Johnny Mack of *Get Published Successfully (GPS)*. And, thank you to the development team with which you've surrounded me.

Thank you all so much! If I missed someone, please blame it on my head, not my heart.

Again, be safe, be vigilant and be blessed.

# We Made Plans

Made in the USA
Middletown, DE
19 November 2020

23778777R00097